BLACKBIRD

HART'S RIDGE

KAY BRATT

BLACKBIRD

A Hart's Ridge Novel

Printed in the United States of America

First Printing, 2024

ISBN: 979-8-9879668-6-0

Red Thread Publishing Group

Hartwell, GA 30643

www.kaybratt.com

Cover Design by Elizabeth Mackey Graphic Design

RED THREAD
PUBLISHING GROUP

This book is a fictional dramatization that includes one incident inspired by a
real event. Facts to support that incident were drawn from a variety of sources,
including published materials and interviews, then altered to fit into the fictional
story. Otherwise, this book contains fictionalized scenes, composite and
representative characters and dialogue, and time compression, all modified for
dramatic and narrative purposes. The views and opinions expressed in the book
are those of the fictional characters only and do not necessarily reflect or
represent the views and opinions held by individuals on which any of the
characters are based.

BOOKS BY KAY BRATT

CHAPTER 1

*L*ife was strange. One day you're going along, and everything is fine—or at least your definition of fine at the time, minus the usual challenges that just being human throws at you—and then suddenly it's upside down and the only friend you have is a blackbird.

For the woman trapped in the confines of a dark and dingy room in a madman's basement, life had become a delicate balance between hope and despair. Every day, as the first rays of sunlight filtered through the tiny window high above, she would wake up and remind herself to stay busy. It was the only way to keep her mind from slipping into the depths of despair. To push away the dread of a visit from him.

Domnus.

The name meant master, he'd told her.

Her response was a blank stare.

It infuriated him.

She lived for the visits from Blackbird. He heard her move with the chain from the other side of the window and knew she was a prisoner. At the close of their visit, he'd lift his head and raise his wings a bit, then call out loudly as he looked around.

Conk-la-ree, conk-la-ree ...

It looked and felt like he was trying to tell someone she was there, to come rescue her and release her from her concrete prison. The woman often found solace in the melodious songs he sang, as if the blackbird was an embodiment of her longing for freedom. But as much as she wanted to reach out and touch him, their connection remained intangible, restricted by the invisible barriers that separated them.

She didn't know exactly how long she'd been there. Somewhere between eight months and a year. On occasion, he drugged her and, when she awoke, she felt it could've been hours or days. Her hair, once cut in a short style, was now long. But then it had always grown fast. Over the last months, she'd learned to live in the present, to focus on the few tasks that kept her occupied within the confines of her room. Staying busy became her means of survival, a way to drown out the eerie silence that pervaded the space around her.

She had crafted her own routine, eventually finding purpose in the simplest of activities. Each morning, she meticulously made her bed, smoothing the wrinkled sheet and fluffing the faded pillow that graced the soiled mattress in the corner.

It was a small act, but it gave her a sense of order in the chaos of her situation.

Then, she would set about cleaning her meager surroundings. With a makeshift broom fashioned from discarded clothes and a broken broom handle, she would sweep away the dust and debris that had accumulated since her last cleaning session. It was a never-ending battle against the grit and grime, but it gave her a semblance of control over her environment.

Afterward, she stood at the small, barred window, watching as the outside world moved on without her. Nothing much happened on the ground. A random squirrel. A dog walking by.

But the sky always changed.

The sky was her canvas. The clouds her paint and the tool that allowed her imagination to take flight. She would discover stories in their makeup, imagining what it would be like to be part of that vibrant tapestry again.

In those stolen moments of reverie, she would lose herself.

Time became her enemy and her ally, as the days blended into one another. She marked the passage of time with the growth of the morning glory vine she'd found behind the discarded wardrobe cabinet. Once just a tiny green bud, it had found a way in through a crack at the foundation, dipping in from the ground level and then raising its head inside.

She tended it with care and watched it thrive under her nurturing touch. It reminded her of the resilience of life, and she drew strength from its steady growth.

As each day would draw to a close, the music would start, and sometimes it was then that he would come.

She'd resisted at first, but he'd broken her spirit after he'd broken bones. A nose that would never be straight again. A wrist that had healed awkwardly.

Pain was a mighty convincer.

The will to live wasn't easily squashed.

Especially when she had children waiting for her to find her way home.

The music became her refuge, a way to escape what he was doing to her body. She would close her eyes and let the notes carry her away, imagining herself dancing freely in an ethereal realm beyond the prison walls.

And so, she danced. In her imagination, away from the dimly lit room, with the stench of his scent threatening to suffocate her, she twirled and swayed, her movements graceful and fluid, as if she was performing on a grand stage. With closed eyes, she envisioned herself surrounded by an audience, their applause echoing in her ears, a reminder that she was more than just a prisoner.

In those moments, she could transcend the confines of her physical space and the abuse. The room transformed into a vast ballroom, adorned with sparkling chandeliers and ornate decorations. She was no longer a captive but a radiant performer, charming the hearts of those who watched her with awe.

Sometimes, she would choreograph intricate routines, mapping out the steps in her mind as she danced. Each movement became a rebellion against her captivity, a declaration of her indomitable spirit. She would leap and spin, her body a vessel of expression, defying the limitations imposed upon her.

As the music swelled within her, her heart soared, and, for a moment, she would forget the bleakness of her reality. In the realm of her imagination, she was free. Free to express herself, free to dream, and free to hope.

But, inevitably, he would finish, and the music would fade. The applause would cease, and she would find herself alone in the darkness once again. The room would revert to its oppressive reality, and the weight of her confinement would settle upon her shoulders.

The guilt and horror of what he'd done to her was always left in his wake.

Yet, despite the crushing despair that threatened to engulf her, she clung to the fragments of joy she found within her daily activities. She knew that was not just a means of distraction, but a lifeline that kept her spirit alive. It was her way of asserting her humanity, refusing to be reduced to a mere captive.

And so, she would continue to rise each day. Continue to make her bed, and clean her surroundings. She would continue to lose herself in the simplicity of a bird, a plant, and the swatch of sky she could see from her window. She would mark each day with purpose, carving out moments of solace and defiance within the bleakness of her existence.

As long as she could stay busy, if she could hold onto the fragments of her true self, she believed that there was still hope. Hope for rescue, hope for freedom, and hope for a future where the songs of the blackbird would be joined by her own voice, lifted in triumphant harmony.

And in the depths of her captivity, she whispered to the departing blackbird with unwavering determination, "Thank you for not forgetting me."

CHAPTER 2

$\mathscr{T}$aylor Gray-Stone wasn't a fan of the local Dollar General store. As a county sheriff's deputy, she'd been called to their parking lot way too many times for petty crimes like loitering or harassment or having to go inside to handcuff a shoplifting suspect. Shopping there wasn't usually a thing. But today she felt the need to stop in when she passed by, so she did a U-turn.

She'd been on patrol all morning, and a cold drink sounded good.

After grabbing a cold bottle of water and a Snickers candy bar, she got in line behind a young mom who was struggling. The mom was trying to pay for two small packs of diapers, a pack of pull ups, and a carton of milk with three gift cards, and the cashier was none too happy with it. The mom held a crying infant over her shoulder, while constantly glancing down to make sure a towheaded toddler was still within sight.

"Mama, I want," the little girl cried out, pointing to a pack of M&Ms.

"No, Chelsea. Not today," the mom said, then turned to reach down and pull her daughter closer. "We must hurry. We've still got to go drop off the trash, and, anyway, you've got candy at home."

Taylor never forgot a face, though she often couldn't think of their names.

"Hi," she said. "Remember me?"

The mom turned and looked at her, a perplexed expression before realization dawned on her.

"Oh, hello. Yes, aren't you the officer that came to give me a noise citation but ended up cleaning up my apartment and taking care of my baby while I showered?" She looked embarrassed and juggled the infant to the other shoulder.

"Yep, that was me."

"You have three dollars and twelve cents left on that card," the cashier said.

Thanking her, the mom took the card and slipped it into her purse, then began putting her bags in the shopping cart.

"Here, let me get that," Taylor said. "You have your hands full. I'm sorry, but I can't recall your name."

"Allison. Allison Curran. Thanks. I appreciate your help. Chelsea is adding to my stress, and just getting her to go to the car peacefully is going to take a miracle. Toby is an angel compared to his big sister."

"Are you a policeman?" the little girl said, looking up at Taylor.

Taylor knelt to be face-to-face with her. "Yes. But I'm called a deputy because I work for the sheriff's department. I met you when you were a little baby, like your brother."

The girl stared at Taylor, obviously captivated.

"Come on, why don't we help your mom get the groceries to the car?" Taylor said, then took hold of the cart handle. They didn't really need a cart for the small number of groceries, but it was a way to divert her attention. "Chelsea, you stand on the end of the cart, and I'll push you out to your car."

"Oh, you don't have to do th—" Allison began.

Chelsea jumped onto the end of the cart, the candy forgotten.

"It's fine," Taylor said, laying her items on the counter. "I'll come back in for my stuff."

Allison led the way outside to a dingy blue van. She opened the side door and climbed in with the infant, putting him into the safety seat. She buckled him in, then climbed down.

"Come on, munchkin," she said to Chelsea. "You're next."

"I can do it myself" Chelsea muttered as she climbed up and into her toddler seat.

Taylor put the groceries onto the floor of the front passenger side while Allison made sure Chelsea was secured. She could smell the bags of trash from the back and winced. Dirty diapers mixed with whatever else was in there was an overwhelming stench. She started to wonder why Allison didn't have her trash picked up but remembered that city pickup cost money.

The little family was obviously not in a position for luxuries like trash pickup.

"Thanks so much," Allison said when she'd climbed down and slid the door shut.

"You're welcome. Be safe." Taylor took the cart while Allison went to the driver's side and got in.

Taylor was nearly at the corral when she heard Allison try to start the van.

It didn't turn all the way over.

Allison tried again, then again. Third time was a charm because it started up—but only did so with a high-pitched squeal.

Taylor wasn't very confident that it wouldn't go dead when they stopped at the trash dump. She waved at Allison, signaling for her to wait.

Allison rolled down the window and Taylor approached.

"What's going on with your van?" she asked.

"I just had the alternator fixed in it," Allison said. "I hope the guy didn't screw me out of my money because I can't afford any more repairs. I just got into a small house last year when I got my tax refund and it's so much better than the apartment, but it's more costly, too."

Taylor remembered that Allison didn't have a partner back when they'd first met. It appeared her luck hadn't changed in the love department. The girl was probably still going it alone, trying to raise two kids now instead of only one.

"I'm not great with motors, but I know a few things," Taylor said. "Pop the hood and let me take a look."

Sam had been doing his best to teach both Taylor and Alice more about vehicle maintenance and repairs, insisting that every woman should know their way around a car more than just the interior. Alice had even perfected the ability to change a tire in under six minutes. She was still counting down the years and months until she could get a license.

Allison popped the hood, and, when Taylor peered under it at the motor area, she didn't see anything out of place. She could see that the alternator had been replaced, though.

"Shut it off," Taylor called out.

"I'm afraid if I do, it won't start again," Allison said, coming up beside her.

"I have a battery booster if it doesn't. Go ahead and shut it off."

Allison went back and cut the motor.

Taylor poked and prodded a few things before she noticed that whoever had put the new alternator in had forgotten to tighten the swing arm assembly that holds pressure on the belt.

"Here's your problem," she said, then went to her patrol car and got a few tools.

She had it tightened in a few minutes, but she noticed that the belt was looking worn out.

"You're going to need to get that changed soon," she said, pointing it out to Allison.

The long sigh that came in response said a lot. It told Taylor that Allison couldn't afford a new belt or someone to put it on, either. She'd been in that kind of position herself one too many times when she was just starting out. Even without having kids to make it more stressful, it sucked to not be able to afford to keep your car in good running condition and just piece it together day-by-day.

"I tell you what," she said, turning to her. "My husband is a mechanic. I'll take a picture of this one, and you come by next week and he'll put it on for you. No charge."

Allison looked relieved. "Are you sure? I can maybe buy the belt if I can borrow some money."

"No problem," Taylor said. "He probably has an extra lying around in his shop anyway. Just come by. Bring everyone and you can meet Alice, my stepdaughter. She's great with kids."

"Wow—thank you," Allison said. "I must ask though. Did you marry that handsome cop that was with you when you came to my apartment? Is he your mechanic?"

Taylor chuckled. "Nope. That was Detective Weaver, just a colleague. I married a man who likes to get his hands dirty." She closed the hood of the van and nodded toward the doors of the store. "I'm going to go back in there and wash my hands. How about Sunday? Come out at noon and have lunch with my family. We're just a bunch of hooligans. Nothing fancy, so don't be shy about it." She gave her directions to the farm.

When Allison nodded and drove away, Taylor could see her blink back the tears that had gathered in her eyes.

Taylor went inside and used the restroom to clean the grease off her hands, then paid for her things and returned to her cruiser. She thought about Allison and other young women like her who got caught up in relationships too young, usually with bad boys who didn't have a lick of sense and wouldn't stick by them. Inviting a near stranger to her home wasn't something she did often, but, if she could get to Allison before she met another bad boy, or before she got pregnant with yet another baby before she was stable, then it would help restore her faith in the younger crowd just a little bit more. Right now, they all seemed to have lost their minds.

She drove up toward the elementary school and parked on a side street. It was her day to watch for super speeders through a school zone and she wanted to be ready.

Allison was nothing like Lucy, other than they were close in age.

Lucy was giving Taylor an ulcer these days, too. Currently she was refusing to speak to their sister, Anna, because of something said that Lucy felt was disrespectful of her newfound career.

Anna hadn't meant anything by it, and Taylor had to agree it was hard connecting the new Lucy to the one they'd always known, and sometimes they thought her success was too good to be true.

In the year since Lucy hosted the art showing for Faire Tinsley, she had gathered more than a handful of clients, some of them very successful. Her little sister was coming into her own, it seemed. She'd broken up with Shane, insisting he was only using her to make Taylor jealous, a ridiculous notion because Taylor was a married woman now.

Shane was her unofficial partner at the sheriff's department, and that was all.

Lucy had taken over Taylor's cabin, because Anna had taken her settlement from her divorce and built a modest new home for her and the kids. It was at the back of the farm, so they were all still together—Cate and Ellis just across the woods—and Taylor had moved back into her own house, with Sam and Alice.

The past year of them living together on a full-time basis had flown by and everything about it felt right. They'd gotten married right after the holiday bustle had ended, picking a date in late January. Sam's father had footed the seed money to build a garage next to the house so that Sam could do his mechanic work there. It was nice having him as an extra hand with the animals, too. Their boarding business was flourishing, and they'd added perks like *walk through nature* or *swim in the lake*, for additional costs. It was shocking how many dog owners would fork out extra money to know their pup was also living like on a vacation at the same time they were.

They still took in animals at their rescue, as well. Taylor wished that Sissy could see all the good they were doing in her name. Margaret brought Hayley out often to see the animals, and it always made Taylor so sad to see the sweet little girl without the mother who had loved her so dearly.

Hopefully Payton Howe's life was miserable behind bars.

The school bell rang out and, from her car, Taylor watched the kids dispersing out the doors, separating like ants to find their way to the buses, their parents' cars, or to the street to walk home. They looked like ants, all of them with a mission.

Taylor looked at her watch. She had to be back to the department in an hour to fill in for dispatch. Dottie was semi retiring, and they still hadn't found anyone to replace her in the afternoons.

Everything was so busy and Taylor's first year as a newlywed had flown by. Luckily, things in Hart's Ridge had settled down regarding crime and so much tragedy. They all still grieved over the loss of Lydia, and Taylor even hiked the Amicalola Falls once or twice a month, still looking for Lydia's remains. A few months after the search was called off, they'd found the strap of the purse that both Barnes and Fisher claimed would be at the site, around the tree they'd left her tied to.

But no Lydia.

It was surreal that, in the year past, they couldn't find any trace of her remains. Either the two were messing with them about the location, or her body had been dragged off by wild animals, what was left of her body lost somewhere in all that rugged terrain.

Caleb still worked, and she saw him nearly every day at the department but seeing him was not a favorite part of her routine, by any means. It hurt her deeply to see how he'd drawn into his shell, letting Lydia's sister and his daughters take over most of the raising of baby Zoey, who was now walking and talking.

Grace and Ella had been forced to grow up too fast, a concept that Taylor was very familiar with and didn't want for them. At least they had Blair, Lydia's sister. She'd left her job as an office assistant to be able to help Caleb with the baby while the girls were in school. Sort of a nanny in that she took care of the youngest, guided her two older nieces on what chores to do, helped with dinner and homework, and then left to spend the evenings in her own home.

She also stood in for Lydia in school events and other things that a mom normally would. Caleb had showed Taylor the prom pictures of Grace, wearing a dress that Blair had helped her pick out. On the nights that Grace and Ella had soccer or volleyball, Caleb didn't even go anymore. He let Blair take Zoey and sit in the stands.

It was so tragic that a mom—who loved her kids as hard as Lydia had—was now missing so much of their lives.

Or perhaps she wasn't.

If Heaven existed, Taylor had no doubt that Lydia was an angel to her daughters, always watching over them, guiding from above. She was probably knocking elbows with Sissy, and that thought made her smile.

CHAPTER 3

*C*aleb Grimes was a broken man. He stood in front of the bathroom mirror shaving, looking at every spot on his face other than his eyes. He was ashamed of himself and didn't like who he had become in the last year. He tried to hide it from the girls, but they weren't fooled; they knew he was just going through the motions.

When he was dressed in his uniform, his belt and gun in place, he went into the bedroom, passing by the bookshelf that still held framed photos of Lydia, along with dozens of her books. She loved to read. Sometimes she read aloud to him, sharing her favorite parts of a book or passage, late at night when they were in bed. That was when she wasn't binging on true crime episodes. He used to tell her she was scheming on how to kill her husband without getting caught. They had that kind of relationship—lots of teasing and laughter.

Yes, he'd married up, that was for sure. Lydia was whip smart. When he'd first met her, she was already successful. Then she'd built her practice, and her patients loved her. She enjoyed what she did, but she'd not once complained about it when they'd decided together that she'd stay home with the girls, and he'd be the sole provider.

He regretted asking her to give up such an important piece of herself.

Finally breaking his gaze away from her photo, he left the bedroom.

The girls were still in their bathroom. He could hear them arguing over the curling iron as he passed on his way to the kitchen.

"Good morning," Blair said as he entered.

"Morning." He went to the table and sat down, taking his chair next to Zoey's highchair. She'd already made a mess of her oatmeal and was in the process of smearing it around as though she were using it as paints, making a masterpiece.

"Zoey," he said. "Is that really necessary?"

When she looked up with her toothless grin, he smiled back. She looked so much like Lydia that a pang went through his heart.

"Kitty," she said, just as clear as day.

Caleb looked behind him and saw that, yes, the cat was strolling slowly into the kitchen. Zoey was fascinated with the cat, but the feelings weren't mutual. Zuri wasn't a fan of Zoey's tight little fists on the rare times she braved walking near her.

Blair brought over a plate of eggs and bacon, toast on the side, and set it in front of him along with a mug of steaming coffee. "I know you don't like a big breakfast, but will you please eat it? You're getting way too thin."

He sighed. Blair was right. Over the past year, he'd lost thirty pounds. He no longer ate for pleasure. It was purely sustenance because it made him feel guilty to enjoy anything without Lydia there to share it with. He wouldn't even touch his old favorites.

Pizza. Food from Mabel's Den.

Both of those were off limits.

"Thank you," he mumbled, and picked up the fork.

"Are you taking Ella to dance class this afternoon?" he asked Blair.

"If I can get her to go. It's getting harder each time. She says it reminds her of her mom too much. I told her that Lydia would want her to continue, and dance for her."

Caleb swallowed hard and blinked back the rush of tears. He couldn't let Blair see him being so weak.

Zoey picked up her spoon and banged it loudly on her tray.

"No, Zoey," Caleb said gently, then reached over and took her spoon and laid it down.

"No, no no no …" she babbled. "No, Bear."

She had mastered several words now, and occasionally even strung them together in a short sentence.

Lydia had missed a lot of firsts.

Zoey's first words. Her first steps.

She called Blair *Bear*. Caleb was thankful that Zoey hadn't tried to call her Mama.

Their youngest toddled around the house now, getting into everything. Caleb didn't know what he'd do without Blair's help. And the girls—they'd had to grow up too fast to be fair. Though they struggled through their own grief, most of the time they pitched in to help with Zoey. Especially at night when Blair went back to her own home.

Except lately, Grace was struggling.

Blair said it was the age, but Caleb wasn't so sure. Grace had her driver's permit now, and, in a few weeks, she'd be eligible to get her full license. She was already pushing for him to buy her a car, but, with what had happened to Lydia, he didn't want the girls to be driving anywhere alone so he was stonewalling both saying yes to the license, and the car.

He wasn't good at reasoning with Grace. He'd always left that to Lydia, who had a way of being both a disciplinarian and their friend. At least he still had some time before Ella would start in on him about a longer curfew, and driving, and everything else that went with getting older.

A car horn blared from outside, and it triggered a stampede down the stairs. Grace and Ella ran in, grabbed a pop tart and juice box each, then started to run out.

"Hold on," Caleb said, putting his hand up. "What's the rush and who is that outside?"

"My friend, Dad," Grace said, her irritation at being held up evident in her tone.

"What friend? Name, please," he replied. "You can't just hook a ride with anyone. I need to know who you are always with. Or you can just keep riding the bus."

"It's Natalie James," Ella said. "She's a senior at our school."

"He doesn't need to know that," Grace said, giving Ella a slight push. "Can we go now, Dad? Please? She's going to get mad."

"Only if you send me her contact info right now," he replied, his jaw set so she wouldn't argue. Grace was a junior at the school and shouldn't be hanging out with the older crowd.

His daughter pulled her phone out with jarring, awkward moves and practically punched the keys needed to send the contact from her phone to his before continuing to the door.

"Goodbye kiss, please," Caleb said.

Grace kept going, the door slamming behind her, but Ella stopped and plopped a kiss on his forehead.

"Love you, Dad."

"Love you, too, Ellie Bear. Have a good day at school."

And she was gone.

That left him, Zoey, and Blair. And too much volume in the room to fill without the big energy of his teenage daughters.

Blair came and pulled out a chair, then sat down, coffee in hand.

"Going somewhere fancy?" he asked, noticing for the first

time that she was wearing more makeup than usual, and her hair looked different somehow.

"Nope. Just making more of an effort. I get tired of looking my age," she joked.

Neither Blair nor Lydia looked their age. Blair always said it was their good Italian genes. He didn't comment about it, though. His relationship with Blair had always been only surface-level, and at times she and Lydia didn't get along.

Usually after a few weeks of cooling off, they were fine, and Caleb didn't ever claim to understand the relationship between sisters.

Since Lydia's disappearance, he was seeing a new side of Blair. She was a lot more caring and selfless than he'd thought her to be. Lydia would be proud of how she'd stepped up for the girls.

"You're not going to eat that, are you?" Blair asked, nodding at his plate.

"I'm going to try. No promises." He pushed a piece of egg around.

"You know, Caleb," she said. "She's been gone a year now. You're going to have to try to live again. Lydia would want that. I know she would."

He sighed heavily, putting his fork down.

"Yeah, I know. I'm not trying *not* to live. It's just so hard." He wanted to tell her that, to him, Lydia didn't feel gone, and they were so close that wouldn't he be able to feel it if she was?

Blair reached over and put her hand on his.

"I know it's hard. And I think I know a way to make things easier for you and the girls."

He looked up from his coffee.

"Since I'm here so much anyway, it might be better if I just move in," she continued. "I can sell my place and help you out with the bills. You won't have to take so much overtime and can be available more for the girls' sports and outings. Have more time with Zoey, too. And I know you're lonely, Caleb. So am I. I was thinking that it could be a win-win situation for all of us."

Caleb didn't know what to say, but he slowly and carefully pulled his hand out from under hers and set it in his lap. Helping them out was one thing, but officially moving another woman into Lydia's place was another.

CHAPTER 4

*I*t was past midnight. Lydia knew that by where the moon was in the sky. She couldn't sleep, as usual. Dom had not come, and her anxiety was high, thinking what if he was detained or in an accident? What if she was left to die there, chained to a pole as she eventually perished from dehydration or starvation?

In her fist she clutched her one earring. When she'd awoken in the basement that first day, she'd noticed that one was gone. She'd taken out the other so that Dom wouldn't notice and try to track down the other.

Lydia had no idea if she'd lost it in the Walmart parking lot, or in Amicalola, but she was relieved to have the other one.

She only took it from under the mattress where she kept it hidden when she knew Dom was most likely asleep for the night. Then she slept with it in her hand, holding on to her last remnant from her life with Caleb. He'd given her the earrings on their first anniversary.

She hadn't worn them often, keeping them for special occasions, but she'd put them on the day she'd gone Christmas shopping. It was a day that seemed decades ago now. She'd left the house feeling festive and grateful to have time to herself.

Then her life was turned upside down and her children were left without a mother.

Because she wanted alone time. She regretted it so badly.

Dom was a psychopath. Or—if she wished to be more politically correct—he had ASPD, Antisocial Personality Disorder, as they now called it. But to Lydia, she simply thought of him as a psychopath, whether offensive or not. It had only taken her a few weeks to determine between that or a sociopath.

When she'd given up her practice so many years ago to stay home with her children, she never dreamed she'd be seeing her most disturbed patient one day in the future—with reluctance, of course.

Dom knew she was a psychologist. He'd seen the news report during the searches, and that was one of the reasons he'd gone to Amicalola Falls to find her before the search parties did. He wanted someone he could talk to about himself, but someone who would understand.

Or so he said.

Lydia had thought she'd die out there in the woods, and his finding her tied to the tree at first was nothing but relief. He said he was part of the rescue team, and helped her to his car, supposedly to take her straight to a hospital.

Only a few miles later, the rag came over her mouth, and she was knocked out until she'd woke in his basement, a shackle around one ankle to remind her that it wasn't a nightmare. She was really kidnapped.

Not once, but twice.

What were the chances? She'd survived the harrowing experience with the two buffoons, Barnes and Fisher, only to fall into the hands of a psychopath.

What had she done in a prior life that she was being punished for now?

Dom said he enjoyed watching the news reports about her disappearance, back in the early days before the searches were called off. He'd come down and report all he'd learned about her. Taunting her with her daughters' names, the fact that her husband was in law enforcement and still couldn't find her. She stayed strong for the most part, until he'd one day come to talk about seeing her parents on the news—pleading for her return.

That one had done her in.

The difference between a psychopath and a sociopath was that the sociopath was more emotional and impulsive and would show violence at the drop of a hat. A psychopath will sit back quietly and take everything in while planning their next moves. The psychopath would never act impulsively and lay bread-crumbs for anyone to follow because they valued their freedom too much. They were more dangerous than a sociopath because of their intense ability to concentrate on any one subject for a very long amount of time without letting it go. They're cunning and can take years to plan their acts because time isn't a bother to them.

What mattered to them most was getting things exactly right.

Psychopaths weren't usually driven by emotion like sociopaths were, and they kept a long list of grievances in their head, turning ideas over and over as they planned their revenge one day, in a way that would prevent them from being caught.

When she was in practice, Lydia discovered that the corporate world was full of psychopaths. That their charm, arrogance, and callousness helped them climb the ladder quite well. Many of them turned their ability to inspire and lead others into what most would call manipulation on their rise to the top.

Politics, too. Many psychopaths were successful in their rise to the top, more silently gleeful with each stripe of power they earned. With their overblown confidence and lack of empathy, their predatory spirit took down anyone in their way.

Dom was a lawyer.

A perfect position for someone like him.

He even looked like a psychopath, his hands and fingernails immaculate. Hair always trimmed and styled perfectly. Neat, well-fitting clothing. Not a wrinkle in sight.

Everything in order and done for a purpose.

Suddenly, Lydia heard stomping above her, then a string of profanity—and more stomping.

He was angry.

She prayed he didn't come to her that way.

Sometimes he only came to talk. Or at least to have her listen since she wouldn't speak back. He obviously loved hearing the sound of his own voice and he talked about his "average" child-hood, poking fun at the studies that said psychopaths had suffered abused lives as children. He told her his parents weren't abusive and that he still had a good relationship with his father. That his mother was a kind and upstanding woman who taught elementary school before she retired and used her gifts for Sunday School after retirement. That his father spent a lot of time with him, teaching him many tools for life.

"Just in case you're wondering," he'd said. "I was born like this. It had nothing to do with how much nurturing I did or didn't get."

He declared that the studies about psychopaths were skewed, and that the entire population of psychopaths was stereotyped because the studies usually involved only the relatively small percentage of those they could interview in prison.

"Those aren't average psychopaths, Lydia. Those are men who ended up incarcerated because of their bad upbringing, or lack of education. Their propensity for drugs and lack of self-control. They have trauma that combines those traits with psychopathy. But men like me, well-adjusted men, we are careful. We are all around you, working beside you or as part of your average dinner party. We're smart and we find ways to get what we want that doesn't involve breaking the law. Or, at the least, we don't act on impulse, that everything is carefully planned out because we don't wish to spend our lives behind bars. There are many ways to get what we want, be it sex or drugs, admiration, or even taking someone's life. The experts don't get to interview men like me."

She'd turned away then, his statement about incarceration bitterly ironic to her, considering her living space and the metal around her ankle.

Only when she'd ceased giving him attention that day had he gotten angry and turned her around violently, making her face him.

"What I did learn in my childhood, though," he'd continued calmly after a few deep breaths, "is that poor behavior is usually excused if one feigns guilt. The other important thing for you to remember here, Lydia, is that you can't make someone *not* a psychopath, but you can help them hide that part of themselves to live as normal of a life as they desire."

His lecture had put a rock of hopelessness in her stomach. If he acted as normal in his outside life as he claimed, there would be nothing to suspect, and no one would ever think to look for her in his clutches.

It would be up to her to find a way to escape.

Someday and somehow.

Her attention was jarred back to the present day when she heard the first lock being slid over, then another, before a deadbolt was turned and the door opened.

Dom stood at the top of the stairs, but she could only see his silhouette. He held something in his arms. A bundle. A substantially sized one, at that.

Lydia's blood ran cold. She cried out when he tossed the bundle, and it hit a few stairs down, then rolled the rest of the way.

The door slammed and Dom was gone.

She told herself to move, not to magnify the fear. Not to let that energy grow into panic. Over the last months, any tiny flicker of anxiety could develop into fear, then a terror that would physically manifest and render her paralyzed into inaction.

At times, she'd discovered that the strength of her fright was out of sync with the reality before her. She knew this, yet it took her a full five minutes to move, to break out of her frozen state before she approached the bundle.

She knelt, squinting in the dim moonlight to see what it was.

COME MORNING, Lydia washed herself, wincing when she gently wiped at her ankle, then changed into one of the large shift dresses. The old wardrobe cabinet was her savior. In addition to a few odds and ends, it held old clothes, discarded or forgotten items from a woman who was twice her size, but Lydia was thankful that she had something to wear. She'd always had a small frame, but she could tell she now looked skeletal because of the weight she'd lost.

Her muscles were aching more than usual, a usual physical response from the deep state of fear she'd felt the night before. The bundle that Dom threw down the stairs had turned out to be a large oval rug. She'd found the source of his anger, smelling the dog urine right after her rush of excitement at having something to lay down upon the cold, concrete floor.

The dog was new. When Dom brought it home, for just a minute Lydia let herself think about Zuri, her cat. Soon after, she felt sorry for the dog who had been unfortunate enough to be chosen by Dom. There was a lot of yelling and stomping the first week, and she'd heard a few yelps, as if the dog had been kicked, then a door slam and silence.

She tried not to think about it, because there wasn't anything she could do, but she did wonder where the dog was kept while Dom was at work, because she didn't hear it during those long stretches.

A dog or cat would be good for company, but that would be cruel. Everyone needed something to give affection to and Lydia had made a small rag doll from stuffing a shirt with more cloth, then cinching out the arms and legs with pieces of another ripped shirt. It was basic, looking more like a Voodoo doll than anything anyone would want to love on, but the nights were long, and the doll gave her something physical to cling to when she couldn't get Zoey out of her mind.

At times, Lydia kept it swaddled in a sweater and talked to it, holding it, and rocking it to sleep as though it really was her baby girl. She was embarrassed, but it brought her comfort.

And she hid the doll from Dom.

The slight sound of the water being squeezed from her rag, back into the bucket, was deafening. Other than the sometimes-muffled sounds from above, her world consisted of so much silence now, such a contradiction of the life she'd been pulled from, one with teenage girls and a baby, always something loud happening around her. She'd never known how much depth and power silence contained. In the silence she found many sounds she used to ignore, or not even hear.

Her heartbeat startled her at times, reminding her that, despite her circumstances, she was still alive. Her intuition introduced itself, too. When the wind wasn't howling, her intuition was on point. It talked to her, calming her mind, or letting her know to get ready, that he was coming. Too bad she hadn't known to listen to it when she was snatched from the Walmart parking lot.

So many things she discovered in the silence. In it she found strength, letting it cleanse her as she listened to her own heartbeat or breath.

She used the water now to wash the long shirt she'd removed from the day before, swishing it back and forth, around and around, before wringing it out and hanging it over the cabinet door to dry, the drip-drip-drip giving her something to listen to.

She remembered the times when her long, busy days were done, and all her girls were in bed, when she padded through the house, going to each room, and standing in the doorways, checking on the gifts God had given to her. Watching them sleep, their troubles from the day forgotten in their innocent slumber.

Never had she thought of the evil waiting just outside her door. How, in one second, she could be ripped from her children, leaving them unprotected.

Now she knew, but it was too late.

Well, they had their father, but he had failed to find her. Surely now he would be more vigilant with their children. She couldn't go there in her mind, to the possibilities—or the thoughts—of what could happen to her girls, like had happened to her, or it would consume her.

She slipped a large gown over her head, then braided her hair.

Right now, at home, Caleb would be up and getting ready for work. A shower. Shave. Then two cups of coffee with two pieces of buttered toast. He never wavered on his routine.

She didn't want to think of him.

The girls would soon be up, arguing over bathroom space. Ella might be struggling to put her hair up in a tight bun if it was her day for class. Her middle child was her dancer, and watching her move gracefully around the floor was one of life's most precious gifts.

Never stop dancing, Ellie Bear.

The other bucket was her toilet. In the cabinet, she'd found an old cloth hair cap like people used to cover curlers on their head at night. She used it to cover the bucket until he came to take it every few days. It was pushed into the furthest corner from where she slept, a dismaying visual reminder of the depths to which her life had fallen.

Her hair was so long now. Longer than she'd had it throughout her marriage. When she and Caleb had started dating, she'd cut it to her shoulders, and he said he liked it, so she kept it that way.

Turning to the rug, she felt torn. On one hand, she was thrilled to have it. On the other hand, Dom had never given her anything nice.

What did it mean?

She went to her washing bucket and wet her rag. She began to scrub the rug, concentrating on the spot of urine.

With the light of the day, Lydia could see that it was beautiful —and obviously expensive. It stunned with a mix of ivory, gray, and copper hues, making up a pattern of pale blue diamond shapes with flowers the colors of fall leaves woven throughout, adding the first bit of color to her dwelling. She smiled, and, when she'd scrubbed the spot as much as she could, she ran her fingers up and down the lines on the rug's pattern, tracing each one until she grew tired.

Dom's internal requirement of perfection was her good luck. She now had something to help with her boredom. Something to use to pass the agony of time.

The human mind that was once, many thousands of years ago, satisfied with simple things, now thrived on novelty. With advancements in the society, the mind yearned for something new and exciting all the time, easily tiring of doing the same thing.

People wanted constant stimulation. Entertainment.

When her daughters used to tell her they were bored, she would remind them that boredom was a reminder to explore new things. To experiment, using what creative energy they could find. She'd tried to get them interested in drawing and painting, like she had been during her childhood and college days. Grace had the gift, just like Lydia's, but she was too immature to care, discarding it for things more common with teenagers.

Social media. Netflix. Boys.

In some cultures, boredom was used as a pathway to self-awareness, but she was already more self-aware than she'd ever been in her life.

Slowly, stretching them out, she did her chores. Taking care to use the old sock to dust every surface, the broom to sweep, and a T-shirt to shine the bottom part of the windowpane that she could reach.

Finally, when she could find nothing else to do, she lay on her mattress. It wasn't yet time to cloud watch. That was for when the sun was the highest in the sky, letting her know that half the day had passed. Then she could look.

And wait for Blackbird.

Keeping to a schedule made her feel like she had a bit of control in her life.

Dom was angry the night before, and she dreaded seeing what he came up with as punishment for whatever crime she didn't commit, yet would be blamed for. His scapegoat.

She only had one act of rebellion that remained, and it enraged Dom.

From the very minute she'd awakened to find she'd been taken she hadn't spoken a word. He had ranted at her, telling her to talk, to say his "chosen" name, to beg for mercy.

Yet she refused.

She did talk, however. When he was gone, she spoke to Blackbird, and to Glory, her vine. It was barely a whisper, just in case Dom was listening at the door, so she kept her words quiet.

At night, when the last of the light was gone and she was thrust into total darkness, she talked to her family, sending messages out through the universe.

I love you. I miss you.I hope you are safe.

Remember me.

Her husband and children were the only humans she allowed herself to think about. A firm believer in manifesting, she saved all her energy for those who needed her the most. In her dreams, other family members popped in and out, and she missed them, but to allow them space in her "awake" conscience would take away from her girls' space. From the bandwidth of what she had mentally to give or send out into the universe.

Sometimes her sister, Blair, slipped into her thoughts.

Knowing Blair, she'd probably stepped forward when Lydia first became missing. Blair liked to be in the spotlight, but she hadn't been much of a supportive sister through the years. It wasn't as bad when they were kids, but, as adults, Blair never could get her own life together, and she hyper focused on Lydia's, her envy showing in passive-aggressive compliments or criticisms.

Lydia always welcomed her into her life, trying to give her the stability she couldn't find on her own, but Blair never showed any appreciation. Still yet, Lydia wished she could see her … embrace her … and urge her to be happy, to see that she was healthy and free. To stop envying Lydia's life and put more effort into building her own.

The sound of the large piece of furniture—or whatever it was —being moved, and then the jingling keys, echoed through the silence, signaling Dom's arrival.

The locks sounded and the door creaked open. He stepped inside, his presence filling the opening at the top of the stairs with an air of malevolence as he slowly came down. He was still dressed in his work clothes—nice slacks and a button up shirt. Shiny, black shoes.

Without a word, he carried buckets in each hand and set them down, then took the other ones back with him, stripping off the hair cap and tossing it aside.

He went upstairs, then returned with a gallon of water and a package of raw wieners that he tossed at her before leaving again. She felt her stomach groan at the sight. Though she was glad to have food, when he brought the wieners, they never set well with her, and she'd inevitably spend a lot of time on the bucket for a few days, the rigid plastic of the rim cutting into her backside.

She wished for something green. Fresh vegetables. Fruit.

Those wishes led to thoughts of pure white milk, or tangy orange juice.

But she wouldn't ask for any of it.

That would please him too much.

He stood over her now, his arms crossed over his chest as he glared down at her. "You're looking especially sorry today," he said.

He bent and examined the cuff around her foot and shook the chain to test it. She saw his expression change when he spotted the wound on her ankle.

"What is this?"

She stared at him, but flinched when he touched her foot.

He took a key from his pocket, and she held her breath in anticipation. He quickly disengaged the padlock on the cuff, then opened it and switched it to her left foot.

Her spirit fell quickly at the click of it being locked again, though it was tinged with relief that the sore would have some respite from the metal.

He looked closer at the wound, his grasp of her ankle brutal and unyielding, as though he was examining the limb of a farm animal.

"Looks infected," he said. "Keep it clean."

She had been keeping it clean, but—with the metal of the cuff constantly chafing it with the weight of the chain—it wouldn't heal. She had no ointment. No bandages. She was afraid of what he'd do if he saw that she'd ripped up some of the clothing in the room. Unlike the doll and the makeshift broom, he'd see it as soon as he saw her.

What more did he expect?

He left again and, when he returned, he held a book tightly, as if it were a sacred text. Her pulse quickened and she struggled to keep the hope from her eyes.

"This world is on the brink of collapse, and only the strongest and smartest will make it," he declared, his voice laced with somber authority. "This book holds the key to survival. If you want to secure your future with me, you'll study it."

She couldn't help the excitement that raced through her. Not for the thought of a future with him. No, her hope was for something more immediate.

Would he really leave it with her?

Without warning, he threw the book hard, and she covered her head too late, and the corner hit her sharply in the forehead.

A flash of pain instantly rushed through her.

But she didn't care.

He'd given her a book.

A book!

She picked it up and looked at it, its title boldly emblazoned across the cover:

"When All Hell Breaks Loose: The Essential Survival Guide for the Twenty-First Century."

In the time she'd been there, she'd learned that Dom was a man consumed by his doomsday obsessions, his eyes gleaming with a twisted sense of purpose as he ranted about things like bridge collapses, hurricanes, pandemics, tornadoes, and terrorist attacks, painting a picture of a world descending into chaos. He believed that the time was nearing when society would crumble, and only those prepared would have a chance at survival.

He pulled a pencil from his pocket and threw it, too.

She almost cried with gratitude, but she hid her emotions.

Lydia wasn't the type to believe the world was teetering on the edge of catastrophe, and she would've wished for different reading material, but she could hardly complain when now she would have something to feed her brain and fill her long hours.

"You see," he continued, his voice growing more animated with each word, "this book holds the secrets to thriving in the face of disaster. It will teach you how to navigate through the darkest of times, providing practical knowledge that will be vital for our survival."

Our survival.

That word piqued her interest. *Our. Our survival ...*

She listened attentively, her mind grappling with conflicting emotions. On one hand, the prospect of acquiring knowledge that could potentially save her life was tantalizing. But, on the other hand, his intentions were laced with sinister undertones, and his words were a reminder of the gravity of her situation.

"Read it. Learn it."

With that, he left her again. He went out with a grand production of noise, slamming the door, locking it, then pushing back the obstacle that blocked it. All the while mumbling about how the whole world was going to shit.

Her fingers trembled as they grazed the cover. Opening it, she flipped through and found herself immersed in a world of doomsday scenarios, survival tactics, and precautionary measures. The pages were filled with instructions on everything from building shelters and sourcing clean water to foraging for food and basic medical skills.

As she delved deeper into the book, she realized that its contents held a peculiar mix of practical advice and outlandish notions. The author's obsession with the impending collapse of society was evident in the fervent warnings and alarmist language scattered throughout the text.

Finally, she closed the cover.

Tomorrow she would start at the beginning and limit herself to one chapter a day.

Smiling, she lay her head down on her pillow.

A book.

She was so lucky.

CHAPTER 5

*O*ver the last few years, Taylor had learned a valuable lesson. It didn't matter what you called it—a network, a clan, or even a tribe—but having a family was a gift, and everyone needed one, whether they wanted to admit it or not.

Thankfully, Sunday dinners were moved to a new location, following Anna to her new house since she was the self-appointed head cook. They all contributed in some way, either bringing food they'd made at their own homes or helping Anna once they got there.

Taylor was done with her dish, and it was staying warm inside a crock-pot. She'd made her famous Swamp Gravy from a few fish that Levi and Teague had caught off the dock. She'd picked up the recipe long ago from a foster home.

It was a great way to make the fish they'd caught—as kids—stretch, like mixing the grease drippings with tomatoes, potatoes, and okra.

Or whatever else they had at hand to put in the hearty stew.

The first time she'd made it she was only twelve years old, and her sisters were hesitant, but, when you had an empty belly, your fussy palate tended to change.

Now it was a family favorite for everyone other than Anna, who still tended to be on the picky side. Sam and Ellis had offered to cook hot dogs and chicken wings on the grill to accompany the fish, for those who weren't fans of eating fish.

Anna was doing the fish to keep it separate.

"What's the best way to tell when the burgers are done?" Sam asked Ellis.

"Meat thermometer, always," Ellis said. "Another tip is to only flip them once. Turn them too much and it'll dry out the meat and make 'em tough."

He was the unofficial grill master and Sam was hoping to learn from him.

"How long do you cook each side?" Sam asked.

"Three minutes for medium-rare, four for medium, and five minutes for well-done."

Taylor sat on the porch and watched them. Corbin stood with the guys, but he seemed more preoccupied than usual, Hank lying near his feet, watching every move.

Diesel had tried to urge Hank into playing, but Hank wasn't having it. He had turned into the best service dog for Corbin, always there if a panic attack started to brew.

The kids were all running around, taking advantage of no homework and being out in the fresh air as they went from the barn to the pasture, then down to the lake and back.

Alice was the oldest and most responsible of the kid group, and Taylor was thankful that she stayed with them to keep an eye out, especially to watch over Johnny. He was always into something.

Anna and Cate were in the kitchen, along with Sutton, who was whipping up her famous potato salad. She and Corbin were like family now, and they attended most every Sunday lunch.

"She's really done something special with this place, hasn't she?" Jo asked.

"Not shocking," Lucy muttered from where she sat on the other side of the porch.

"I think it is a little bit shocking," Taylor said. "Or I guess surprising that she didn't go too big or too fancy. Anna has really changed. I'm happy for her that she's put all that stuff with Pete behind her."

"She's going to make a fantastic nurse," Jo added. "No doubt she'll be running the place wherever she ends up once she's done."

"The other nurses will salute when she comes down the hall," Lucy said.

They all laughed, thinking it wasn't too far from the truth.

Anna had decided to get off the career track she was on when she'd married Pete. He'd insisted any wife of his didn't need to work. Recently his fancy lawyer had gotten him out of serving jail time, but ironically Pete was now broke and unemployable in the legal field, so his mistress-turned-girlfriend was supporting them both.

Turns out that the other-woman didn't end up with the rich attorney she'd thought she was getting. Now she had to babysit him and pay the bills!

Taylor couldn't wait to see the day that he had to eat humble pie and get a blue-collar job. He'd always looked down on anyone else who didn't wear a suit and tie to work. She'd once asked him how he thought the world would run without tradespeople who fixed plumbing, dug wells, and built houses. The only blue-collar work that Pete ever seemed interested in was law enforcement, and he liked to question her as to what was going on in the department and any new cases or arrests. Probably looking for clients.

Anna didn't mention Pete much anymore, and the kids still didn't want to see him. However, Anna was mediating video calls between them and their dad, because she claimed, one day, they might appreciate that she tried to keep their father in their lives.

The *Gray Escape Pet Boarding* would be fine without Anna at the helm full time, at least that's what Taylor told Cate. Anna would continue to help them with the business administrative duties, but it would be part time so that she could pursue the career she felt passionate about. Animals weren't her thing, other than the two dogs she'd adopted.

Cate had given her full blessing and said she just wanted her girls to do whatever made them happy.

Their mom was back to full duty and couldn't be happier. Now that she and Ellis were living together in their new home, he helped a lot on the farm, and she wore a glow on her face whenever they were together. He'd sold his houseboat and bought a pontoon, and he and Cate went out on the lake nearly every night in good weather. They claimed it was for Brandy, their dog, but it made Taylor smile to watch how in love they were.

A chorus of barking alerted them that someone was at the gate, and they all turned.

Taylor recognized the van immediately.

"Oh, that's a new friend," she said. "I invited her to lunch today. I'll get the gate."

She waved at Allison, then walked down to the gate and opened it, letting her drive the van through. But Allison didn't drive all the way up the drive. She stopped just inside the gate.

Taylor went to the driver's side.

"Hi, Allison. You can pull up—" she stopped when she saw Allison's face.

"Sorry," Allison said, putting a hand up to cover the area around one eye, "I don't want to come up, but I need a favor and I don't have anyone else I can trust."

"What happened to you?" Taylor said, fury going through her as she imagined the beating the girl had taken.

She looked over Allison's shoulder and saw that Chelsea was

staring at her wide-eyed, like she was in shock. The baby was asleep in his seat.

"It doesn't matter, and I know this is a huge ask, but do you think you could keep the kids here tonight? I drove around from place-to-place last night while they slept, but I don't have the gas money to do that again, and we can't stay at my house. I can sleep in the van somewhere."

"Allison," Taylor said. "Listen to me. You need to file a report on whoever did this to you. We can put them in jail so that you can go home. Was it Toby's dad?"

Allison looked away, but a tear slid down her bruised cheek.

"Please, Officer Gray," Allison said. "I don't want to talk about that."

"Taylor. Just Taylor. We're friends, Allison. Let me help you." Taylor could see her family on Anna's porch, looking down the drive curiously.

Allison turned back to her. "You don't understand. I've been through this before with Wyatt. I file a report. He gets arrested. I get a no contact order and he bails out, then breaks the order. He finds me and then I get it worse for putting him in jail. A piece of paper means nothing. I just have to hide out and wait for him to cool down. But I'm out of places to go where he won't look for me."

Taylor shook her head, trying to think of what she could say to convince Allison that whoever beat her needed to be prosecuted. But she could see in the proud lift of the girl's chin that she wasn't going to give in, so she was going to have to take a different approach.

"Have you ever stayed in a domestic violence shelter?"

Allison shook her heard. "No. I didn't know that Hart's Ridge has one."

"That's good. It's supposed to be a secret. If everyone knew about it, then the women wouldn't be safe there. Come on up to the house and let me call and see if they have room for you and the kids. Just until you can think straight."

Allison looked like she was thinking it over. She peered into her rearview mirror, looking at her children.

"You have to think of them, Allison," Taylor said. Chelsea still hadn't said a word. "They shouldn't see things like that. They'll be protected at the safe house."

Taylor could easily take them all in and even protect them. But the safe house wasn't just a shelter. It was a place that other women who had survived domestic abuse talked to those still in the thick of it. They were the best examples, showing that it is possible to get out and move on to a better life. Allison needed that. Also, the director and owner of the house was a special woman that everyone in town loved. But most of them only saw her in her public role and had no idea of her passion and secret vocation of helping the victims of domestic abuse.

"Okay, we'll go if they have room," Allison said.

Taylor squeezed her arm. "Good girl."

"But I don't want to meet your family like this," she added.

"I understand. Just drive on by the house where you see my family on the porch, then my house is the next one on the left. I'll walk up and meet you. Take the kids on in and make yourself comfortable. I'm going to grab some food for you and the kids. I'm sure you're hungry."

Allison nodded, and Taylor could see a new sheen of tears come up.

It was hard to accept kindness when your soul felt broken.

※

TAYLOR PULLED her car down the long, winding driveway, flanked by trees whose branches reached out as if to embrace those who entered. Up ahead, nestled among the foliage, stood a grand old two-story house. Its weathered, yellow exterior spoke of years gone by, yet it exuded a sense of warmth and comfort, for she knew what lay within.

"This is it," she said, pulling up to a big, black, iron gate.

A hand-painted sign hung on it, a beautifully painted black and white tower.

The Lighthouse

It was a fitting name for the place that Mabel used as a sanctuary for those who needed it most. Taylor keyed a few numbers into the pin pad, and the gates opened.

Allison didn't say a word.

She sat still as a statue, as though her body was frozen.

As they went through the gate and parked, Taylor glanced in her rearview mirror at the children. Her heart clenched at the sight of Chelsea's solemn face peering out from the back seat, her face curious and a bit nervous.

A memory of another girl came to her.

Despite the different hair color, Chelsea reminded Taylor of Molly, and Allison was just like Molly's mom, doing the best she could to be a good mom, despite life's hurdles.

Jodi, Molly's mother, never got a chance to see what she could be. Her life was snatched from her too soon at the hands of a man.

But Allison—she could be saved if she'd only let others help guide her.

Taylor stepped out of her car and opened the door for Chelsea, unbuckling the traumatized child, while Allison got Toby out of the infant carrier.

They were met on the porch by Mabel, who concentrated on Allison and enveloped her in a tight embrace, her comforting presence a balm to the wounds both seen and unseen.

"Oh, I *know* you," Allison said when she'd pulled back.

"Yes, I own The Den. I believe you and your kids have been in a time or two to eat," Mabel said. "If I remember right, your little girl is a fan of my Friday night chicken fingers, though the baby isn't old enough to sample much, yet. What's his name?"

"Toby," Allison said. "And Chelsea."

Right on cue, the baby let out a frustrated cry and Allison bounced him up and down to quiet him, but he wasn't having it.

"Allison, dear, come on up and sit down," Mabel said, her voice a soothing melody. She took Toby and expertly put him over her shoulder, patting him on the butt. "We need to have a conversation before we move forward."

As they settled into rocking chairs, Mabel soon had Toby sleeping, his cries silenced by her expert touch. Allison looked like a scared rabbit, ready to bolt at the first sight of an enemy.

Taylor listened as Mabel began to outline the rules of her place, each word spoken with a mixture of compassion and resolve.

"No photos, no divulging our location," Mabel said firmly, her gaze unwavering. "But you're safe here, Allison. You and your children."

Taylor interjected, her voice firm with conviction. "The security here is paramount. We can't risk anyone finding out about this place."

"I understand," Allison said.

Mabel picked it up again. "That also means you can't take a taxi or ride share here. You can't get a food delivery. You can't have visitors. If you come and go, you'll need to be picked up and dropped off somewhere that is far away enough to make it hard to figure out the location. If you have a car, park it elsewhere."

Allison nodded, her eyes shimmering with unshed tears. Chelsea, suddenly oblivious to the weight of the moment, giggled as she chased after a butterfly that flitted by.

"Her van is at the farm," Taylor said. "It can stay there as long as needed."

Mabel continued, her words a lifeline in the storm of uncertainty. "So now let's talk about *inside* the house. A cluttered or messy environment breeds a cluttered and messy mind. We strive to keep that from happening while you are recovering, or just catching your breath. This is a big house, and you'll have chores, but you'll also have support. We're a family here, Allison. And we take care of our own."

She emphasized the importance of attending support meetings, of sharing burdens and finding solace in the company of those who understood what she was going through.

Taylor watched as Allison's resolve wavered, her gaze shifting to her children, who were too young to understand the situation, but old enough for it to still affect them years down the road, especially if Allison didn't stay away from her abusive boyfriend.

"Mama, I want to stay here," Chelsea piped up, her small voice filled with innocence and trust.

"Well, young lady," Mabel said. "That's going to be up to your mama. I might be the queen of this castle, but she's still in charge of you and your brother. Allison, what do you say? Want to try us out for a bit?"

Even a child could feel the warmth and safety that Mabel had created there.

Allison's breath caught, her heart laid bare in that moment of vulnerability. With a quiet nod, she whispered her acceptance.

Taylor felt a wave of relief wash over her, knowing that Allison and her children were now under Mabel's watchful eye, surrounded by walls that whispered tales of hope and healing.

They were silent, and, as the sun dipped below the horizon, casting long shadows across the porch, Taylor knew that, within these walls, amidst the creak of rocking chairs and the soft murmurs of support, if Allison gave it a chance, she might find the strength to rebuild her life, one brick at a time. And she would not have to do it alone.

CHAPTER 6

*C*aleb sat at his desk in the sheriff's office, the soft glow of his computer screen casting a pale light across his solemn expression. He scrolled through Facebook with determination, his mind preoccupied with ensuring the safety and well-being of his daughters. His fingers moved with purpose as he searched for information about Natalie James, the girl who had picked them up earlier that morning. He needed to make sure she was trustworthy, that Grace and Ella weren't catching a ride with some hooligan.

As he clicked through her profile, scanning posts, then on to her father's page, Caleb couldn't shake the heaviness and fear that weighed on his heart. He looked at family photos taken at a campground, at a skiing resort, and one that appeared from a church directory.

They seemed like a decent enough family, but Caleb was still wary.

He was terrified that something would happen to the girls. So scared, that every minute he wasn't with them felt like an hour, obsessing that he wasn't there if something should go awry. He was gone a lot, too. The guilt wracked his mind, the tug-of-war between being with his girls and still doing what he could to find closure for Lydia, always going on inside him.

It was only because of Blair that he let them out of his sight at all. She and her constant efforts to get them all back to normal. He appreciated her and wasn't blind to the fact that she was basically the one holding them together as a family.

He went to Amicalola Falls every weekend. Not only to search, but also to talk to Lydia, but it still felt hollow. Sometimes he'd take the girls with him, hoping to feel Lydia's presence among the trees and rushing water. Other times, he'd go alone, seeking solace in the quiet solitude of the forest, falling to his knees as he begged God to make the hurt go away.

But no matter how hard he tried, he couldn't shake the feeling of emptiness that seemed to follow him everywhere.

He glanced over his shoulder as he heard footsteps approaching, and Taylor appeared beside him, her presence a welcome distraction from his troubled thoughts.

"How's it going, Caleb?" she asked, her voice warm and friendly.

Caleb managed a small smile, though it didn't quite reach his eyes. "Hey, Taylor. Just ... you know, checking up on a few things."

Taylor nodded in understanding, her gaze lingering with a hint of concern. "Everything okay?"

He hesitated for a moment, debating whether to confide in her. But something in her kind expression encouraged him to talk.

"Yeah, I ... I've just been thinking too much lately," he admitted, his voice tinged with sadness. "About Lydia, and ... everything."

Taylor's expression softened, and she placed a comforting hand on Caleb's shoulder. "I know it's been tough. Losing Lydia ... it's something none of us can fully understand."

He nodded, grateful for Taylor's understanding. "Yeah. I've been going up to Amicalola Falls every weekend, you know?

Sometimes with the girls, sometimes alone. But ... I just don't feel her there, you know? And ... I don't feel anything when I visit her grave, either."

Taylor listened quietly, her gaze filled with empathy that made him wince. He felt pathetic. Less of a man because he'd let his wife down when she needed him the most. Even more aware that he was letting his children down, too.

"It's okay to feel lost, Caleb. Grief is a journey, and everyone travels it in their own way."

Caleb sighed heavily as he shared his burden with Taylor. "I know. It's just ... hard."

Taylor gave his arm a reassuring squeeze. "I understand."

He turned his chair around to face her completely. "I did want to ask you about something, if you have a minute."

She pulled up a chair from the desk next to him. "Shoot. Ask me anything."

He squirmed in his chair before letting it out. "It's about Faire Tinsley. I just wondered, well—" he trailed off.

"I'm sure she'd be glad to talk to you, Caleb," Taylor said.

Caleb's brow furrowed in uncertainty. "I just don't know. I've never been one to believe in that kind of thing." He looked around, rising tall in his seat to see over the cubicle wall, before whispering. "I don't want any of the guys to know if I decide to talk to her. I'd never hear the end of it around here."

Taylor offered him a small smile. "I get it. I was skeptical, too, at first. But Faire ... she's different. Just give her a chance. It might be just what you need."

He nodded slowly, a sense of resolve settling over him. "Thanks, Taylor. I appreciate it. I think I might go by there on my lunch break, see if she's around."

"Anytime," she said, her tone filled with sincerity. "And, hey, if you're a bit late coming back, I'll cover for you."

Caleb managed a grateful smile, feeling a sense of gratitude for Taylor's unwavering support. "Thanks. I've got school patrol today, but I should be able to make it. I'll let you know if I need you, though."

With that, he rose from his desk, his mind made up. He was going to find Faire Tinsley, and, perhaps, with her words, he would find the guidance and solace he so desperately sought to help him move on from Lydia's tragedy.

FROM THE STREET, Faire Tinsley's home was practically shining, soft lights on in every window. With the success of her art, many pieces bought from customers all around the world, and others being commissioned faster than she could keep up with, Caleb saw that she'd put a good bit of coin into restoration and renovation of the large estate. Not a moment too soon, either. The home had begun to look forlorn, forgotten for so long when it came time for a refresh.

Pots of bright red geraniums graced either side of her front door, set off even more by the sharp, new black shingles on the house. The once patchy lawn now looked as soft and green as a lush carpet.

He pulled into the long driveway and parked next to Faire's new car, a cheerful, yellow Volkswagen bug, one of those with the flower bobbing on the dash. It fit Faire's personality perfectly, and he couldn't help but smile when he saw her driving around town in it, her bird perched on her shoulder proudly.

Seems that Faire Tinsley finally got the stardom back that she'd once turned away from. The locals in Hart's Ridge were very proud of her and respected the fact that her newfound celebrity status did not keep her from running the summer camp she and Della Ray had started the year before. More and more of their local kids were learning real life tools that couldn't be taught on TikTok or Instagram but came naturally from two women who had spent years perfecting things like how to whip

47

up a quick-but-hot breakfast, how to stack a dishwasher correctly, and ways to turn a quick buck while helping neighbors. Manners and respect for elders and authority figures, with role-playing to show them how a decent person interacted with others in those roles.

That was Caleb's favorite part of their curriculum, and he'd sent Grace and Ella for a five-day workshop when he heard they included it. And Grace had learned to balance her first checking account.

All the things that Faire and Della Ray were teaching now were once familiar to everyone but had been lost in the rush to modern times.

The door was propped open by one of the planters, and Caleb stepped inside. There was a couple in the hall, standing and gazing at one of Faire's paintings. He didn't recognize them as locals. More than likely from Atlanta or somewhere around there. They looked up and nodded, then bent their heads together, speaking quietly in a tone that sounded very pleased with what they were looking at.

It appeared Faire might have another sale.

He went on through the hallway to the parlor, and Faire was sitting on a stool in front of an easel, filling in a sky with a pale shade of blue. Her bird was on her shoulder, as expected.

"Deputy Grimes," she said, turning to smile. "What a nice surprise."

"Just call me Caleb, Mrs. Tinsley," he said, nodding respectfully.

"Deal. Then you must call me Faire." She stood and put her brush into a jar of milky water, wiped her hands on a small towel, then came to him and embraced him, squeezing hard. "I haven't had a chance to tell you how sorry I am about Lydia. I did attend the service, but you probably don't remember much from that day."

Caleb looked around, scoping out where the couple was, then

seeing them climb the stairs to where Faire had added another small display area.

"That's—that's kind of why I'm here, actually. I'd like to talk to you about my wife. If you have a minute, I mean."

"Of course I do." She took his arm and led him over to the velvet couch, taking the chair next to it. She rubbed her hands together, looking to him expectantly.

Caleb didn't know where to start. He felt so awkward.

"Taylor said I should come here. She said you might be able to help. Or—or, something. It's just that Lydia has been gone more than a year now and I still haven't been able to feel her around me. I talk to her all the time. At home, in my car, and up at Amicalola. You would think that I'd feel *something*. I just don't."

Faire sighed heavily. "And you want to know if I can connect with her."

Caleb held his hands up. He should've followed his usual skepticism. This was a waste of time. "Well, no, not if you aren't comfortable with it. I mean, I could pay for your time. Or I could just go—"

"Oh, Caleb," Faire said, smiling gently. "It's not that I don't want to mediate a conversation between you and Lydia, it's just that I can't."

He was confused.

"Mrs. Tinsley, I really need to find Lydia's body. I want to bring her remains home, so she can be at peace. So that I can be at peace, too. Thinking of her lost somewhere in all those woods is driving me crazy. I feel like I'm losing my mind."

Faire leaned forward, cupping her hands under her chin with her elbows supported by her knees. "You aren't going crazy, Caleb. You are just in pain. And I'll tell you something else; usually when people walk in here with someone heavy on their mind," she continued. "I immediately get something. You see, Lydia's spirit should be going everywhere with you. At least until you've come to peace with her passing and she can break that invisible thread and move on to her next journey. But when I looked up from my painting, you were alone."

"I don't understand," he said. "Does that mean she's okay? That she's not hanging around me because she is fine with her death? She's on to another— journey?"

"It could mean that, sure," she nodded. "Sometimes spirits just do not want to be bothered by anything from earth. They do have a lot going on, you know. They're planning their next lessons. But—and I don't want you to take this wrong, or get upset—have you considered that Lydia might not be dead?"

His mouth nearly fell open.

Two things hit Caleb all at once. One was how easily and nonchalantly Faire used the word *dead*. The other was that he thought she was supposed to be a medium, not a mind reader.

CHAPTER 7

*J*ust as the sun began to set across the water, casting a warm golden hue over the tranquil lake, the final guests arrived, and they were ready. The gentle lapping of water against the wooden dock created a serene melody, setting the perfect stage for the intimate wedding about to take place.

Surprisingly, the few rustic benches the men had set out were now full, saved for the guests who came from outside the farm, like Cate's friends from the Humane Society, and Ellis's kids. The sheriff and his wife had come, too, though Taylor could tell that he was antsy to get back to work.

She stood with Sam, Alice, and Diesel between them as they watched Cate and Ellis standing side by side on the wooden planks of their dock. Adele standing in as the maid of honor.

"The string lights look fantastic, Jo," Anna said.

They really did, the twinkling of the soft lights reminded Taylor of the lightning bugs they chased when they were kids, before Cate went away. Now they had them back, along with the whole family, and it felt like they had come full circle.

"Adele looks as proud as a peacock," Sam said.

Taylor laughed. Her grandmother acted as though she was fully responsible for her daughter's newfound happiness, and that was okay. She'd been through a lot, too. She'd also just lost her little dog, Prancer, and was holding it together well for today.

Cate had made the comment earlier that she was waiting for a special dog to come along at the farm to give to Adele, once she'd grieved her dog long enough.

"They almost planned the ceremony at the dock where they met, but Cate wanted it here behind their new home," Taylor whispered to Sam. "She thought it would be special, and more private."

She couldn't get over how radiant Cate looked, her long hair twisted up into a French knot, soft tendrils framing her face and her makeup barely-there-but-lovely applied. Even though this was her mother's first real wedding, she'd chosen a slim, off-white vintage gown of understated elegance. In her hands, she carried a delicate bouquet of wildflowers. Each of her grandchildren contributed to it—a project guided and put together by her newest addition, Alice.

Ellis looked comfortable and classy in a cream-colored pair of linen pants and a white shirt that fluttered loose around him.

Cate's shy smile lit up her face as she gazed into his eyes, the man who had become her rock and her anchor in the stormy seas of life. He looked back at her as though she were the most beautiful woman in the world, and to him, she truly was.

Scars and all.

Taylor didn't usually believe in fairytales, but in this case, she had to admit that their story came pretty darn close.

"Ellis, please take Cate's hands in yours," Cecil said. He looked dapper in his suit, and so very proud to be officiating the union. He'd grown very close to Cate, almost as close to her as he was to Taylor, because they spent so much time together in the kennels, working with the animals. He also saw that at her core, Cate was a wounded soul, and that was Cecil's specialty when it came to people.

Taylor loved that he'd been honored this way. Cecil had always been family to her, and it warmed her heart that now he felt that way to all of them at the farm, including Cate and Ellis.

Ellis' weathered hands trembled ever so slightly as he reached out to grasp Cate's, a silent promise of unwavering support and devotion.

"Look at Brandy wag her tail," Alice said quietly. "She thinks this is for her."

Taylor and Sam laughed. Of course they had to have Brandy up there. She was their real matchmaker! But not according to Lucy, who tried to claim the title. Everyone knew that without Cate's crazy adventure to rescue Brandy from her abusive owner, she might never have met Ellis.

On the bank with Taylor's crew, all the family members stood behind the benches. Per Cate's wishes, they dressed simply, khakis and white shirts for the men, and baby blue summer dresses for the women. The children went barefoot, pants rolled a few times on the boys and old-fashioned sundresses on the girls.

Corbin and Sutton were there, too, along with Hank, always at his master's side.

Anne's dogs, Mutt and Jeff, ran around, dipping in and out of the water. Lucy's dog, Ginger, rested on the bank, lazily watching everything around her. She'd gained a lot of weight, especially for a Beagle, and looked like a fat sausage.

Diesel seemed to understand it was a special moment, and had resisted his usual urge to jump in. It helped that Sam kept his hand on his collar.

Jo stood nearby, Levi on one side, their dad on the other. All somber as they watched and listened. Taylor was proud of her dad for coming and being respectful, even though they all knew he still loved Cate.

She felt a rush of sympathy for Jo, and hoped that one day soon, she'd meet her real soul mate and her heart would stop getting stomped on. Maybe even Anne, too.

Everyone needed someone to love.

"Let's begin," Cecil said, looking out over everyone.

The children quieted.

"Today, we gather to celebrate the union of Cate Gray and Ellis Cross," Cecil began, his voice resonating with warmth and sincerity. "Their love has weathered many storms, yet it has only grown stronger with each passing day. Today, they stand before us, ready to embark on a new journey together, hand in hand, heart to heart."

The gentle breeze carried his voice to everyone on the bank as he spoke of love and commitment, weaving together words of wisdom and hope for the future.

Taylor felt a lump form in her throat as she listened, overwhelmed by the beauty and simplicity of the moment, and by the wonder that she had brought her mother back home to them after so many years of believing she was dead. Cate had turned out to be the missing piece of their family, and she held them all together.

Taylor couldn't imagine them without her now, and she couldn't imagine Cate without Ellis. They were made for one another, and she'd never seen her mother so content.

As the vows were exchanged, emotions washed over Taylor.

She glanced at Sam, his eyes shimmering with unshed tears, and she knew that they were witnessing something truly magical.

He squeezed her hand, reminding her that they'd already had their moment, and their union too, was forever. Their wedding was just as sweet, and nearly as simple, too. Taylor had never been a girly-girl and she didn't want her ceremony to be a big deal. Her sisters were surprised, though, that she'd decided on a church wedding.

They had all driven up to a tiny, private church outside of

Asheville with just the same people that were here today, minus Cate's friends from the Humane Society, and adding Sam's dad and a few other of his relatives. It was beautiful and Taylor's dress was also vintage, dating back a hundred years. Anna had insisted on bridesmaids' dresses for her, Jo, and Lucy, and a maid of honor dress for Alice.

Anna had her fun with the dresses and Jo the flowers, but they'd kept their word to keep the attire within the simple theme, too, and not make Taylor's wedding into something that would not fit her low key personality.

She and Sam had stayed on budget and the entire affair for their wedding was less than a thousand dollars and twenty minutes, two things that Taylor left the mountains feeling proud about.

Taylor could see that she got the no-fuss-trait from her mother.

"Do you, Ellis, take Cate to be your lawfully wedded wife, to have and to hold from this day forward, for better or for worse, for richer or for poorer, in sickness and in health, until death do you part?" Cecil asked.

"I do," Ellis replied, his voice steady and unwavering as he looked into Cate's eyes with all the love in his heart.

Taylor could see a tear run slowly down his cheek, the last of the sunlight glinting against it to create a diamond effect on his skin.

"And do you, Cate, take Ellis to be your lawfully wedded husband, to have and to hold, from this day forward, for better or for worse, for richer or for poorer, in sickness and in health, until death do you part?"

"I do," Cate whispered, her voice barely audible over the gentle rustle of leaves and the distant chirping of birds.

"I now pronounce you Mr. and Mrs. Ellis Cross," Cecil said, smiling proudly.

With those simple words, Cate and Ellis sealed their vows

with a tender kiss, a promise of forever written in the soft caress of their lips.

Corbin began to play a song on his guitar, the chords and melody soft and haunting. Taylor immediately recognized it as *Woman*, by John Lennon, her mother's favorite musician.

Ellis and Cate turned to the crowd, smiling triumphantly, and the children took off to dance, explore, and just be kids. The dogs took that as their release, and Diesel made a beeline for the water, splashing those next to the edge as he jumped in.

Over the music, they all laughed.

"The food's ready at the house," Anna called out. "Last one there is on dish duty!"

That made the kids drop everything and race toward the house, laughing and pushing to get ahead of each other.

The sounds of family.

It all felt so good, and Taylor was glad she'd been able to compartmentalize everything she had going on with work, so that she could stay in this moment, and have this memory. She didn't usually let herself feel any pride, but she suddenly had an epiphany. If she hadn't pursued the truth about what had happened to Cate, and then fought for her freedom, they wouldn't be standing here now.

Her family wouldn't be complete, and Ellis would still be living a lonely life out on the water, having sworn off ever finding love again.

And as the sun finally dipped below the horizon, she knew that this moment would be etched in her memory forever, a testament to her ability to always look for the truth, because it could bring about miracles.

CHAPTER 8

"*L*et's see," Dom said, sitting in the chair and crossing his legs in a feminine way. He opened the book on his lap. "What can I learn about myself today?"

Lydia stared at him, her expression blank. She'd figured out that was the best way to deal with him when he was in a mood like this one. Even the twitch of a muscle in her face could set him off. Anything he felt was an indication of a bad attitude was forbidden.

Despite his mood, he'd brought her a special treat, he'd said.

A Hershey's chocolate bar. It sat next to him on the mattress.

Lydia tried not to look at it too much. To taste it would be wonderful, but the memories attached to just looking at it were brutal. Ella was always the one to beg for a Hershey's chocolate bar when they were in line at a store.

It was rare that Lydia could turn her down. If she ever got out of there, she'd let her Ellie have as many chocolate bars as she wanted.

"It says here that psychopathy is marked by an extreme lack of empathy. That we can be manipulative, charming," he looked up and raised his eyebrows at Lydia, smiling. "Oh, and exploitative.

That we often behave in an impulsive and risky manner. Well, that's not true. I'm never impulsive."

She didn't respond.

"Except for one time. When I saw the news report that they were searching the Amicalola area for you. I knew I could find you first, but I had minutes to decide if I wanted to do that," he looked back at the book. "And, yeah, we may refuse to accept responsibility for our actions. My mother tried to tell me it was my fault that my brother killed himself, that I should feel bad. Why would I feel bad when it was his greediness that told him it would be okay to invest into an idea I had. It would've been successful, too, if someone else hadn't swooped in and got the patent first. Not my fault that Kenny lost his life savings. I was smarter and only put in a little. Mom said I lacked a conscience. I suppose that's true; I didn't feel any guilt."

His description was spot on, Lydia thought, though she could think of a few more adjectives for him, and she let them run free in her mind. She thought of how, at times, Dom was gentle with her, and then, with a flip of a switch, he handled her harshly. Afterward, he never showed remorse. He'd never had a guilty feeling in his life, and she'd bet the farm on that.

People tended to throw around the word "psychopath" a lot, using it on ex-spouses, or partners, or even friends and family that they ended things badly with.

Others considered anyone who was deceitful and narcissistic a psychopath. It just wasn't true. It was an ego-driven world full of dishonest and self-absorbed personalities, but that didn't make someone a psychopath.

In the medical world, some doctors found a direct link between someone with psychopathy and the amygdala of their brain showing hypo-activation.

Lydia didn't feel that biology was destiny.

"I suppose that you think all serial killers are psychopaths, don't you?" he said. "Spoiler alert—it's a myth. Everyone thinks we want to kill people. Probably because of our lack of empathy. I won't say whether I fantasize about killing someone or not, but I will say this: I may not have any emotions when presented with the pain of someone else, but that doesn't mean I'll go out of my way to cause pain."

He was right. There was a misconception that all serial killers were psychopaths. Simply not true.

Dom sat back in the chair and again crossed his legs. "How many psychopaths have you had the opportunity to interview, dear Lydia?"

She stared back at him.

"None? Interesting. Perhaps you'd like to take this opportunity to interview me?" he said. "Ask me anything. I'll answer as truthfully as possible."

Lydia was tempted. Psychopathy still interested her. She'd probably spent far too much time watching true crime, homing in on the episodes that she felt involved someone truly mentally ill.

"Don't forget about the chocolate," Dom said, his tone teasing.

He wanted her to talk so badly.

No. She could shrivel away to nothing before she'd trade her voice for food. It was the only thing he hadn't taken from her.

"Cat still got your tongue, huh?" he said, laughing at his own joke.

She blinked, but nothing else. Her face was impassive. She'd learned to stay away from looking at him with any sort of disgust or disdain. It could set him off.

"Remember what I said about being impulsive?" he said. "I'm going to give in to the thought that just popped into my head. You have a conversation with me, and, in addition to this delicious chocolate I'm going to leave you tonight, I'll bring you fruits and vegetables tomorrow."

His words sent a streak of excitement through Lydia, but she didn't show it in the least. Her mouth watered. What she wouldn't give for a piece of fruit—or a fresh salad. There were other things, too, that she craved, like cheesecake, or a Diet Coke, but most of all she wanted clean food. She made herself eat the crap he brought to her, wieners, tins of tuna. Sometimes beef jerky or a burger patty, if she was lucky and he had leftovers from his own meals.

So much meat. She wasn't a vegetarian, but she probably would be if she survived this nightmare.

"No?" he said, tilting his head. "Are you sure?"

He waited a few more seconds, then shut the book on his lap with a loud bang.

She jumped. A reflex of fear that she couldn't help.

But, thankfully, he didn't look angry.

"That's fine. I hope you're enjoying the book I gave you," he said.

More fear.

Please don't take the book back, please don't take the book ...

"I assume you read the first chapters," he said. "If I remember right, chapter one is all about cockroaches and their superb survival skills. I can't say that I'm fond of the little creatures myself, but they can be quite impressive. They've been around for more than four hundred million years, you know. Unlike most other insects, they give birth to their young live, so no eggs to worry over and protect."

Lydia was terrified of cockroaches. They were disgusting little insects. She'd had an apartment in college that kept getting infested, even though she kept her place immaculate. It was because her neighbors didn't care, and their roaches crossed the hall to her home freely. She'd moved out before her lease was up, losing money she couldn't afford because she couldn't stomach going into her kitchen at night.

Dom looked at the ceiling.

"No cockroaches around here, Lydia. They're also known to be quite lazy and are only active about twenty five percent of the day. Laziness is something I can't tolerate. Don't have to worry about that with you, do I? You keep it tidy down here in your little home."

He looked all around before his gaze fell on the mattress that lay on the floor.

Please no, Lydia thought. *Not today.*

"But—" he said suddenly. "Back to the book. The next chapter talks about the huge outbreak of fear around the world on the eve of the year two thousand. Do you remember where you were, Lydia?"

She did remember. Caleb thought it was all nonsense (and had turned out to be right) and had swept her away to his favorite sports bar for a few games of pool. They'd only half paid attention to the television during the countdown, though a small part of Lydia was a bit worried that there could be some validity to the nervousness around the world.

Dom scratched at his chin, looking pensive.

"I was in court, earlier in the day," he began, a glint of intrigue in his eyes. "I was prosecuting a corporate case that had the entire tech industry on edge. It was a massive conglomerate against two guys who used to work for them but went off on their own with a small startup. They were fighting allegations of stealing intellectual property that could change the course of their futures."

As Dom recounted the details, Lydia couldn't help but be captivated by the narrative. The case sounded complex and filled with suspense, making her momentarily forget where she was. Her life in the basement was mundane, and, yes, Dom was crazy, but at least he brought her stories from the outside world.

But then, his tone shifted, and he admitted something that took Lydia aback. "You know," Dom confessed, leaning in slightly, "I always knew deep down that those defendants were innocent. The evidence pointed in their favor, and my gut told me they were being wrongly accused."

Lydia watched him preening like a peacock. He was so proud of himself.

"But," he continued with a wry smile, "I also knew that winning that case would solidify my reputation as a brilliant lawyer. So, I played my cards, manipulated the situation, and secured a victory, despite knowing the truth. The small fries lost everything."

The confession left Lydia feeling sick. She was repulsed by his willingness to influence the system for personal gain.

Dom stared at her, then he picked up the chocolate bar and tucked it into his shirt pocket before standing and towering over her, his expression suddenly thunderous.

"I hope you're reading that book, Lydia," he said, his tone turning steely. "I bet you think that I'm some kind of amateur prepper, don't you? You can get over that notion, because there's a whole army of people like me out there—professionals with money, people who know what they're doing. When the shit hits the fan and everyone else in this nation is scrambling around like those little cockroaches we talked about, looking for crumbs and shelter to stay alive, I will be perfectly content in the refuge I built for myself, full of everything I need to keep right on living."

She looked down at the book he'd given her.

"And, Lydia, if you play *your* cards right, who knows ...," he smiled slowly. "I might just take you with me."

He left her then, taking the chocolate bar with him.

CHAPTER 9

*a*llison sat in the circle of chairs, her hands trembling slightly as she clasped them tightly in her lap. She glanced around the room, taking in the faces of the other women gathered there, each carrying their own burdens of pain and fear.

The visiting counselor was Pam Kleiser, a woman with gentle eyes and a reassuring smile. She began the session by acknowledging the bravery it took for each woman to be there.

"We're here to remind you that what happened to you is not your fault," the counselor said, her voice soft but firm. "You are not alone, and there is support available to help you through this."

She continued talking, and Allison listened intently, her heart heavy with the weight of her own experiences at the hands of Wyatt, a man who claimed to love her. She couldn't shake the worry gnawing at her insides, the constant fear for her children's safety, even within the walls of this sanctuary.

Chelsea's dad had left the scene right after his daughter's birth, and Allison was raising her as a single parent until she met Wyatt, who had jumped in and made her believe that he wanted to be a part of their lives. They'd moved in together briefly, she got pregnant, then things went downhill, and Wyatt moved out.

But they were on again, off again, trying to make things work because of Toby. Allison wouldn't let him move back in, though, because he still hadn't shown her that he could be responsible or curb his temper.

Even so, she'd tried so hard to make it work, forgiving him over and over, allowing him access to Toby—and even Chelsea— as they navigated the choppy waters. But this time he'd gone too far.

"It's surreal when you realize that all that time you thought you weren't good enough," Pam's voice broke in, "when the reality is that you were too good, all the time."

The counselor turned to Allison, her gaze warm and inviting. "Since you're our newest member, I'll start with you. How have your first few nights been here, Allison?"

Allison hesitated, her mind swirling with conflicting emotions. She wanted to open up, to release the floodgate of fears and doubts that threatened to overwhelm her, but she couldn't find the words.

"It's been ... different," Allison finally managed to say, her voice barely above a whisper.

The counselor nodded understandingly, giving Allison the space she needed to gather her thoughts.

Because she had two children, Mabel had given Allison her own small room. It had a set of old-fashioned bunk beds, a full bed on bottom with a single on top, both made with colorful lightweight quilts. And there was a crib for Toby. Other than that, there was a desk and a small dresser squeezed against the opposite wall. Only one window, but it looked out over the back of Mabel's property, a gorgeous scene of thick woods with a line of mountains visible in the distance. Gazing out had given Allison a surreal feeling, like she was in the middle of someone else's dream, and needed to find her way home.

Chelsea was excited to sleep on the top bunk the first night but that only lasted until the lights went out, then she got scared and came down to snuggle up to Allison. Toby was still taking an extra-long time to go to sleep, the confusion of the unfamiliar place evident in his crying.

Internally, Allison had wrestled with the urge to flee, to return to the familiarity of her old life—despite its dangers. To let Chelsea have her bed back and Toby to be rocked in her grandmother's antique rocking chair before bed, in a place he recognized. But she knew deep down that she couldn't risk her children's safety any longer. Maybe talking it out would help her the next time she felt weak.

"It took everything in me not to go back yesterday. I woke up feeling so lost and out of place again. I miss my little house. My kids miss their rooms," Allison admitted. "I started thinking that, maybe this time, Wyatt might really change. For Toby, if not for us. He really wanted to be a dad and did so good the first few months with his son. Before things got complicated."

"Life is always going to be complicated," Pam said gently. "It's how we react that makes us who we are. It was just as complicated or more so for you, right?"

Allison nodded.

"But you didn't resort to violence, did you?"

"No, of course not. And I know it's not safe for us there. I was just saying, it's hard. We all miss our routine."

Pam nodded, offering a reassuring smile. "You're doing the right thing by staying here, Allison. It takes courage to break free from the cycle of abuse. You had a bad day yesterday, and that's okay. Some days will test you more than others. Sometimes you'll feel you can rise to the challenge and then other times you need to step back and reserve your strength. Both choices are brave and acceptable."

Allison's heart swelled with a sense of validation, grateful for the support and understanding she found in this place. But it still felt strange to be among people she didn't know, playing house in a home that wasn't hers.

Pam shifted the conversation to Allison's concerns about her job, prompting Allison to voice her worries about maintaining employment while navigating the challenges of starting over.

"I can't work there right now," Allison said. "My manager said that Wyatt has been coming there every day to see if I show up. I'm going to end up losing my job."

Allison unloaded trucks and stocked shelves at Walmart, and she didn't make a lot of money, but they'd given her a full-time position with regular daytime hours and health insurance. She had to really stretch the money, but it was enough to keep the kids in daycare and a roof over their heads. Whatever was left she made stretch for groceries and other needs.

She was happy with her job. There weren't a lot of options in Hart's Ridge for someone like her, with no other experience or higher education, and the store manager had noticed that she was productive and had a way with displays. He'd even mentioned the possibility of her training for a management position one day.

"What about the no contact order?" Pam asked. "Any updates?"

"I'll call again today, but yesterday they said it was on the judge's desk."

As the discussion unfolded, Pam's attention was drawn to another woman in the circle, one who spoke with a mix of fear and defiance.

"I swear, if he lays one filthy hand on my mama ..." she said after she'd introduced herself as Denise. She shared her own harrowing experience, revealing that her estranged husband was now threatening her extended family, trying to get them to give up where she was staying. When she said it had been nearly a year now and he wasn't giving up, Allison's breath caught in her throat, her pulse quickening with a renewed sense of hope-lessness.

At least Allison didn't have to worry about her family. Her father wasn't in the picture and her mama had washed her hands of Allison when she'd come home pregnant with Chelsea. They hadn't stayed in contact since then and Wyatt didn't even know where her mother lived.

Pam offered words of encouragement and practical advice, reminding Allison and the other women of the resources available to them, including legal protections and support networks.

Another woman started to mention the ineptness of law enforcement when it came to protecting them, and she brought up a name that brought all of them to silence.

"Jessica was an extenuating circumstance," Pam finally said. "Her assailant went above and beyond to find her, and she put herself in a position where she couldn't be protected. That's why all of you need to think long and hard before giving in and going back to your abusers."

That was all that Allison was doing these days; thinking. And so far it wasn't getting her anywhere.

CHAPTER 10

*I*t had been a week since Caleb's conversation with Faire Tinsley and, taking a deep breath, he squared his shoulders and knocked lightly on the doorframe.

"Grimes, come on in," Sheriff Dawkins' voice called out, cutting through the tense silence. Caleb stepped into the office, his eyes flickering nervously to Detective Weaver, who sat in one of the chairs opposite the sheriff's desk.

As he took a seat, Caleb felt the weight of the sheriff's gaze upon him, and he struggled to find the right words. "I ... I wanted to talk to you about Lydia's case," he finally managed to say, pushing down the emotion in his voice.

The sheriff's expression softened. "Of course. We're always here if you need to talk about it," he replied gently. "Did you call that number I gave you?"

"No, but thank you. I don't need the counseling. It's just ... I just can't shake the feeling that there's more to it," he admitted, his voice trailing off uncertainly. "More to what happened to her."

Detective Weaver's eyes narrowed slightly, a hint of skepticism in his gaze. "What more is there? Barnes handed us Fisher on a silver platter, said his buddy told him he'd strangled her around that tree. He even led us to their camp. What are we missing?"

Caleb swallowed hard, feeling a surge of frustration at Weaver's dismissive attitude.

"I don't know, Weaver. Maybe a body?" he said, unable to keep the sarcasm from his words. "The girls and I need to have her remains where we can honor them. Visit. Talk to her. An empty grave feels just that—empty."

Sheriff Dawkins exchanged a knowing look with Weaver before turning his attention back to Caleb. "Caleb, we've been over this. Barnes's statement was corroborated by his accomplice. You know as well as we do, when a body is left on a property like a wooded national park, there's all sorts of things that can happen to it."

Caleb winced, visualizing a bear dragging Lydia through the woods, or a pack of coyotes tearing her apart.

"But there is a slim chance that we didn't find her body because she isn't dead," he said, looking at them hopefully.

"Why would someone admit to killing someone if they didn't?" Weaver asked.

Sheriff Dawkins leaned back in his chair, crossing his arms over his chest before sighing loudly. "I didn't want to tell you this, Caleb, but I think it's time. After the search was called off, during the trial, and even well after Barnes and Fisher were sentenced, I had people searching Amicalola. I've sent dozens of hikers up there, and even a few trackers. All on my own dime because we didn't have the budget to keep manpower going. Every one of them came up with nothing. So, you see, there's no reason to reopen the case," he said firmly, his tone leaving no room for argument.

Caleb felt a knot tighten in his chest, the weight of disappointment heavy upon him. He had hoped that the sheriff would understand his need for closure, but it seemed that his efforts were in vain. "I know, Sheriff. It's just ... hard to accept," he murmured, his voice barely above a whisper. "But I thank you for doing that. I can repay you. You shouldn't have to use your own funds. It might take me some time, but I'll start making payments now if you just let me know how much it all came to."

Sheriff Dawkins leaned forward, his expression filled with sympathy. "I don't want your money. Losing Lydia was a tragedy, and it's natural to want answers. Even I couldn't let it go until I just had to. Sometimes, we must accept the truth, no matter how difficult it may be and no matter how many questions are left unanswered," he said gently.

Caleb felt a surge of frustration at the sheriff's words, his heart aching with the pain of loss. "I can't just sit back and do nothing," he protested, his voice tinged with desperation.

"What would Lydia want you to do?" Weaver asked.

Caleb didn't even answer. He knew what she'd want him to do. Lydia would want him to keep looking until he found concrete proof that she was truly gone forever. Weaver couldn't possibly understand the love they had.

Sheriff Dawkins gaze filled with pity. "Look, I know you're hurting. But you need to take care of yourself. Maybe take some more time off, go see a counselor," he suggested, his tone gentle but firm. "I can put in a request for a few more weeks of paid leave. Send it up the ladder and try to get it approved."

Caleb shook his head resolutely, his determination unwavering. "No, Sheriff. I need to work. It's the only thing keeping me from going crazy," he insisted, his voice tinged with defiance.

He also needed access to all his past files.

The sheriff's expression softened, a silent understanding passing between them. "Alright, if that's what you want. But promise me you'll take it easy, alright? Take some time with your daughters. Remember, they need you. Show them they still have one parent here for them," he said softly.

Caleb nodded, a sense of resolve settling over him. "I will,

Sheriff. Thank you," he murmured gratefully, his heart heavy with the weight of his decision.

As he rose to leave the office, Caleb felt a renewed sense of determination coursing through his veins. He may not have the sheriff's support, but he would not rest until he had answers. Even if he had to pursue the truth on his own, he would never give up hope of finding Lydia's remains and bringing them home.

CHAPTER 11

*D*om had left his chair in the basement the last time he'd visited, and Lydia thought that very peculiar. At least until he'd arrived more than three hours ago and tied her to it. She should've known that he never did anything accidentally, or to be nice. Even though she'd enjoyed having somewhere to sit other than her mattress for the last several days, he'd had a purpose that had nothing to do with making her life more convenient.

He'd found a new way to enjoy his sadism. Tying her to the chair made him happy. Seeing the ropes wrapped around her waist and legs got him excited.

He laughed slightly from his place on her mattress. He was reading a book, legs crossed at the feet, ignoring her and her discomfort.

Twelve Ordinary Men, the title read.

Lydia could see the cover very well. Twelve men were dressed in ancient robes, implying that the book was a biblical one, and the men the apostles.

She hadn't made a sound during the three hours he'd been there. Her wound on her ankle stung under the tough ropes, reminding her that, if she wasn't careful, it could get infected, and she could die. More than that, her body throbbed in all the muscles and joints, dismayed at the constant unmoving position it held.

I am breathing.

I am blinking.

I am alive.

The book Dom had given her had touched on the power of the two words, *I am,* and how what followed the words should continue to be positive, rather than negative, to maintain her strength and courage through unpleasant situations.

Dom was trying to break her, and he might succeed.

But not today.

Finally, he shut the book and swung himself around to a sitting position, facing her.

"You know what I really like about you, Lydia?"

She stared at him.

"You don't try to ply me with compliments or promises," he said. "If you submitted to my will, or showed your weakness, you'd be an unworthy adversary and I'd tire of playing with you. As it is, I'm intrigued. I wonder what it is that makes you tick. What keeps you from shutting down."

Lydia's daughters' faces ran through her mind.

"Compliments are nothing more than emotional manipulation. I should know. I'm very good at them. See what I did there?" He winked.

From her career, she already knew that what he said was true, or at least when it came to psychopaths. Positive interaction with a psychopath relied on mutual respect and interests. Appealing to their ego never worked.

Dom claimed he came from a normal family, that he had good parents, but family is a relatively loose term to a psychopath. Family didn't have to be related by blood, and if you were accepted into the family of someone with ASPD, in a sense they felt like they owned you.

In her studies, she'd learned that the psychopath would go above and beyond to protect something they considered to be theirs. Not love, by any means. Simply ownership.

He held the book up, waving the cover at her.

"I bet you're wondering why I'm reading this drivel, aren't you? Well, because you asked," he grinned at his joke, "it's required educational resources for me to fit in where I want to. Did you know that the church is full of psychopaths like me? Hell, even Paul the apostle was a remorseless killer before God supposedly changed him. By his own acclaim he'd persecuted dozens of Christians to death. Yet, no one wants to call him names."

He came to a standing position.

"Your Jesus never shunned anyone, right? Come on, Lydia. Even Paul didn't want to eat with harlots or criminals. My church is full of men like Paul. They might think they are mighty and good, but do you really believe they'd sit down with the dregs of society and break bread? If they were truly dissected, you'd find they lack empathy. They lie and manipulate and have sex with anything that moves. Yet, we worship together, interspersed in and between the real people of God, wolves dressed in sheep's clothing."

No argument from her there. Dom was the biggest, baddest wolf she'd ever come across.

"Religion has its place, though, don't get me wrong. It's a necessary control mechanism for the masses. Christians have a need to believe there's something greater than themselves. Their fear that it could all be a grand hoax—*and it is, mind you*—feeds and fuels religion. Greed nourishes it. Everyone wants to believe in that prize of one more destination once their life is over. A reward for their good deeds. Their faith in the mythical guy in the sky. The greedy megachurch pastors fuel the nonsense even as they are lining their pockets. Those are the true geniuses of the world, don't you think, Lydia?"

She'd never tell him what she thought of it. The fact that her firm trust in God and the strength He provided her was the secret ingredient to her so-far-survival in the hands of a psychopath. That her belief that this journey she was going through was part of her life plan, and had a reason, kept her opening her eyes each morning, rather than succumbing to the easier option of death.

She would never believe his lies, especially about God and the church.

He crossed his arms over his chest, staring down at her.

"Would you like to be free of that chair?"

It took everything in her not to *say* yes.

She nodded solemnly.

"I'll just bet you would, dear," he said. "I think you need some more time there, though. I tell you what; I've got some work to finish upstairs. Getting ready for closing arguments tomorrow. Big case, Lydia!"

He looked pleased. Eager to eat the defendants alive with his words.

"But if I finish early enough," he continued, "I might turn on some music and come back down. If I do, I'll untie the ropes so we can get the most out of our time together."

He meant to make her really suffer under the ropes. Physically and mentally. He might even leave her there all night. Though something told her he'd be back down for more *time together.*

A shiver ran through her, ending in the tips of her fingers that were already numb. She'd rather stay in the chair, under the ropes. The now familiar lustful look in his eyes made it clear what he wanted to do with that time.

CHAPTER 12

*G*oing anywhere from The Lighthouse was complicated,
but it was the first time in the week and a half since
Allison had arrived that she was going to have a
babysitter for a few hours. She wanted to use that time to go by
her house and pick up some more clothes and a few other things.

When she'd finished walking the mile to the corner where two
country roads crossed, she only had to wait for twenty-five minutes
for an Uber driver to show up. She'd chosen a woman driver, no
longer trusting men, even if they did have good reviews online.

Allison climbed in and shut the door, and the driver took off.

It felt good to be out and about, and Allison put the window
down a few inches to let the breeze in. She'd been so busy with
her chores and the sessions at the house that she'd barely been
outside. The driver turned the radio on and sang along with
Chris Stapleton. His rustic and throaty voice was her favorite,
and Allison let herself forget for a moment that her life was in
shambles as she hummed to the words of *Tennessee Whiskey*.

Chelsea had barely nodded when Allison told her she was
going to be gone for a few hours. She was occupied with her new

friend, a four-year-old little girl named Amber who was staying there with her mom. Chelsea went outside with them frequently while Allison used the reprieve from her rambunctious daughter's endless energy to nap with Toby.

Today there was a special visitor coming and giving all the moms a few hours to themselves. A small group of ladies from a local church would be taking care of the kids, reading, and teaching them Jesus songs, Allison supposed.

One had mentioned finger paint and she hoped that Chelsea didn't get it all over her outfit, because they didn't have many for her to wear.

Pam, the counselor, was at the shelter again this morning and when she saw Allison leaving, she'd stopped her. "Not going to be in our session later today, Allison?" she'd asked, putting her arm around Allison's shoulders.

"No, I've got some legal stuff to take care of," Allison had lied. She felt bad about it because Pam was such a nice person, but Allison had promised Mabel that she wouldn't go back to her place until they'd decided it was safe.

The no contact order had come through and was served to Wyatt at work to make sure he got it. He wasn't supposed to be anywhere near the house or her and the kids, until at least the next court hearing.

Allison knew that if he got into any more trouble, he was going to lose his job at the plastics factory, so she felt confident he'd stay away. He had a fancy four-wheel drive truck with hefty payments that was his pride and joy. He needed that job to keep it.

As the Uber car approached her small house in town, Allison's heart raced with a mix of anticipation and dread. Nestled on a quiet street lined with towering oak trees, her home itself was modest, with a weathered exterior that spoke of years gone by. Its soft pastel paint had faded over time, but the welcoming porch swing and flowers that were planted by a previous tenant added a touch of charm to its humble facade.

This was the first place of her own that she was proud of. It had felt like a real home. Not only to her, but to Chelsea and probably Toby, too.

Pulling up to the curb, Allison couldn't help but wish that the last few weeks hadn't ever happened, and that they could rewind time. Stepping out onto the worn pavement, she took a moment to breathe in the familiar scent of freshly cut grass. Someone was always doing yard work on their street. The air felt crisp and clean, a stark contrast to the suffocating atmosphere of fear and uncertainty that had consumed her in recent weeks.

As she made her way up the creaky porch steps, the gentle creak of the swing echoed in the stillness of the afternoon. As she reached out a trembling hand to brush against the peeling paint of the front door, she noticed that there was a letter pasted to the door.

It was an eviction notice, and on it was a small sticky note.

Neighbors called, complained of noise, I came over to find that you've trashed my house. You have 30 days and I'm filing a report for property damage.

With dread, Allison pushed open the door and stepped inside; her senses were instantly on alert. As her gaze swept across the room, her heart sank at the sight of the devastation that lay before her. Furniture lay overturned, belongings scattered haphazardly across the floor, and the once inviting atmosphere now felt cold and desolate.

Her couch was turned over and it smelled strongly of urine. The photos of the kids she'd hung on the wall were now on the floor, the glass shattered.

Tears gathered in Allison's eyes as she took in the extent of the damage, her heart breaking when she spotted her grandmother's antique rocking chair, now resembling a pile of match sticks. That was the only good thing her mother had ever given her.

With each cherished possession Allison saw destroyed, she felt shame run rampant through her.

Mr. Barbary thought she'd done this.

Wyatt.

The shame turned to rage as she walked through the living room and into the kitchen, stepping carefully over the broken dishes strewn about. She peeked through the back door and saw what remained of a bonfire, with remnants of clothing and books showing up between the ashes and charred pieces of wood.

She walked quickly to her bedroom and saw that her bedding was pulled off and in the floor, and her mattress had also been urinated on. He'd been drunk; she knew that instantly.

The photo of her and Wyatt with the kids that was on her nightstand was out of the frame and ripped into tiny pieces.

Allison went to the closet and confirmed what she already suspected. Only bare hangers. There was nothing salvageable in the entire room where she and Wyatt had lain together and planned their future. But it was also the room in which he'd thrown her against the wall, then held her there by her neck until she'd nearly fainted.

She reached up and rubbed at her throat. She remembered how black and cold his eyes had turned as he was choking her. Like he didn't even know her.

She'd seen the devil that night.

She snapped some photos with her phone, then quickly left the room.

She never wanted to see it again.

Chelsea's closest was empty, too, and that really burned Allison. She could understand Wyatt's anger at her, but why at an innocent child?

Where was the man who had promised to treat Chelsea as his own?

This was a new low for Wyatt, and she'd never forgive him for it.

She spotted Pinkie, the elephant stuffie, on the floor and picked it up.

In Toby's room, she breathed a sigh of relief that at least it was untouched. Seems Wyatt had some honor, leaving his son's things alone.

Allison pulled out a few onesies and sleepers and tucked them under her arm with the elephant. Suddenly she remembered the folder of documents and she ran back to the kitchen, nearly falling over the debris in the hallway. She opened the nonworking dishwasher and breathed a sigh of relief as she pulled out the folder.

At least she had their birth certificates and social security cards.

Quickly she went back through the house, taking photos of every bit of damage she could, wanting to catalog it because she'd be filing a report, too.

As she was finishing up, she felt the hair on her neck stand up.

Wyatt obviously didn't care about a piece of paper restricting him from coming to their home or near her. He'd broken the no contact order like it had never been delivered.

What if he was on his way back over there now? Or worse, outside waiting for her?

She hurried and gathered up the folder, the clothes, and the stuffie, then left by the back door. Feeling like a low life thief, she took off running down the alley. She needed to get somewhere else and call for a ride back to The Lighthouse. Things just got a lot more complicated and, now, she and the kids could never return to their home.

Her mother was right; the only thing that Allison could do well was make a mess out of her life. She'd failed her kids again.

She cried as she ran, tears of frustration and self-pity running down her cheeks.

After she'd gone a few blocks, she stopped and hid behind a tree while she fired off a text to the only person she knew to ask for help.

CHAPTER 13

*C*aleb Grimes sat at his desk, his fingers hovering over the keyboard. As he meticulously combed through the extensive database of arrest records, his mind focused on one singular purpose.

He scrolled through the files, his thoughts drifting back to the countless cases he had worked over the past two years. He made a mental note of individuals who had shown animosity directly toward him during their arrests, jotting down their names and any relevant details that could help him track them down.

One name stood out to him: *Daniel Sullivan.*

Caleb vividly remembered the volatile encounter he'd had with Sullivan during a routine traffic stop that had escalated into a violent confrontation and Caleb taking him to the ground, his face slapping against the pavement. He'd resisted arrest, and assaulted Caleb, and, by the time he was sitting in the county jail, he'd racked up a lot of charges, including a felony.

Sullivan had threatened him with retaliation, and, although Caleb had dismissed it at the time, he couldn't shake the feeling that Sullivan might hold a grudge. But that was over two years ago, and surely Sullivan didn't harbor ill feelings for *that* long?

Another name caught his attention: Marcus Johnson. He recalled the heated exchange he had with Johnson during an altercation at a local bar, where Johnson had been arrested for disorderly conduct. The hostility in Johnson's eyes as he was led away in handcuffs still lingered in Caleb's memory, sparking a flicker of suspicion.

It felt like an endless list of people who might hold a grudge.

Lost in thought, Caleb didn't notice Taylor enter the room until she spoke up, her voice pulling him back to the present. "Hey, Caleb. Why are you still here? Shouldn't you be at home by now? It's after three."

He glanced up, offering her a weary smile. "Hey, Taylor. Yeah, I probably should've already left, but ... I've got something on my mind," he admitted.

"What about the girls? Won't they be worried?"

"Blair is taking them to Chick-fil-A. They won't even notice I'm not home."

Taylor frowned as she approached his desk.

"I doubt that's true. What's going on? Something bothering you?"

He tapped the escape key to clear his screen as she came closer. "Not really. Just catching up on paperwork. You know how it is."

"Yeah, I do," she said. "But I also know that you're never behind on yours. Caleb, you can confide in me, you know. Want to tell me what you're doing?" she asked, her tone gentle.

Caleb hesitated for a moment, his gaze drifting back to the computer screen before he finally spoke. "I've been going through old case files, looking for anyone who might have a vendetta against me. Someone who might have targeted Lydia to get back at me," he confessed, his voice heavy with emotion.

"But Barnes already told us that Fisher confessed to him for killing Lydia. I'm confused."

He sat back in his chair, unsure how much to share with her.

He'd noticed since he came to work there that Taylor and Sheriff Dawkins had an unusually close relationship.

"Remember we talked about Faire Tinsley?" he finally asked.

Taylor pulled up a chair next to him.

"Yep. What did she say?"

"Not much. It's what she didn't say that got me. She said she has not picked up any connection with Lydia, and that it could be unusual. Or—it could be that she doesn't want to stay around us."

"I get it. We need to bring her body home and then maybe you can move on."

"That's just it. I don't think Lydia is dead. Nothing has been found of her remains. No torn clothing. And now, Faire can't connect with her? I know I sound like a lunatic, Taylor, but I mean it. I feel like this isn't over. At least not until I bring her home, in whatever form it may be. I am not going to stop until I can give my kids some kind of closure. Just hear me out, please."

Taylor nodded solemnly. "Go on. I'm listening."

"In those first days when we began searching for her, the press was all over it. Lydia and I were splashed on every news channel and people from all over the state saw my face. What if one of them was someone with a vendetta against me? I know this is really out there, but they could've thought right then and there if they could get to Lydia first, before the search party, they'd settle the score."

"That's really reaching, in my opinion. Again, Barnes said that Fisher admitted to strangling her. So, in your scenario, your enemy steals her body and carries her miles out of Amicalola? For what? I'm sorry, but that doesn't make sense to me."

How could he get her to understand? He felt frustration well up in him before he tried again.

"But what if Fisher only thinks he strangled her to death? But she survived? And got loose or someone took her? It's also a reach that two escaped inmates would just happen to escape and drive hundreds of miles before coming to a Walmart parking lot at exactly the same time that Lydia was going to her car, and they carjacked and abducted her. Look at everything that had to happen just right for their paths to cross? Why can't another outrageous scenario play out? It's not impossible. If it was, then I'd let it go. But I just can't."

The energy it took for him to say all that sapped him of every ounce of strength, and he put his head in his hands.

He felt Taylor's hand settle on his shoulder. "Okay, if this is what it takes to bring you some peace, let's do this. We'll start by making a list of everyone you've arrested in the past two years, and then we'll cross-reference it with their current whereabouts," she suggested, her voice brimming with determination. "But you have to make me a deal."

He looked up.

"Once we clear everyone on our list, you agree to take some time off and get some deep counseling. Not just for yourself, Caleb, but for your girls. Deal?"

He put his hand out and she clasped it and shook.

"Deal," he said.

"Good. Tonight, we gather names, then—as we have time this week—we'll track them down."

Caleb felt relief wash over him. Taylor was a Godsend because he knew, with what he was going through, she'd have to take the lead and help him wade through the heavy emotions to get the information they needed.

For the next three hours, they worked tirelessly, meticulously compiling a list of names, and gathering information on everyone. With each new lead they uncovered, Caleb felt a renewed sense of hope stirring within him, a glimmer of possibility that they might be one step closer to finding Lydia.

When Taylor's phone went off, she looked at it and saw photos popping up, one after the other. They were of the inside of a house, but everything was in disarray. She flipped through them.

"What is it?" Caleb asked, sounding concerned.
"It's from a friend of mine. Something's wrong."
Then a text came through. And another.
She read it to him.

> Wyatt's gone crazy. He broke into my house and vandalized it.

Another popped up.

> I'm really scared that he's going to find us.

"I've got to go, Caleb," Taylor said.

CHAPTER 14

*T*aylor was parked at the curb, the afternoon sun casting long shadows across the street. She was waiting for Caleb when she should've been at home with Sam and Alice, getting ready for their Sunday night movie with popcorn. It was her turn to pick the movie, too.

The last few days had been tense. After she and Shane had processed the scene at Allison's house, they put in for a warrant for Wyatt Heaton, and now they waited for it to be approved so that Taylor could go get him and put him in jail.

Allison had promised to stay put with Mabel and let the anger die down before she tried to get out and about again, for her and the kids' safety.

In the meantime, Taylor was splitting her time between work and helping Caleb with research. There wasn't much left over of her waking hours to spend with her family.

To add to the dog pile, Caleb was ready to go talk to a few of the names on the list, and she'd promised, so here she was.

Daniel Sullivan was first, and they had already confirmed that he was out on the street and not serving time during November

10 of last year through the end of the month, at least. That meant that technically he could be a suspect.

Caleb had recounted to her about how a simple traffic stop with Sullivan had turned into a confrontation and a felony. That could be enough for him to hold a grudge, for sure.

She watched as Caleb emerged from his house, a troubled expression on his face. She rolled down the window as he approached the car, concern knitting her brows together.

"Everything alright, Caleb?" she asked.

He got in and ran a hand through his hair. "Probably a good thing you didn't come to the door. It's Grace," he admitted, his voice heavy with frustration. "She's angry with me again. Crying and telling me she hates me. She wants more freedom, but I stood my ground."

"What does she want to do?"

"To go to the mall with some friends this weekend. I don't even know these kids. Lydia never allowed her to go anywhere unless she knew the parents or made a lot of phone calls. Grace won't even let me do that. I can't even send Ella as a chaperone— or spy. Grace says she doesn't want her sister tagging along—and now Ella is mad, too."

Taylor listened sympathetically. "She's acting out the only way she knows how," she offered. "It's been a hard year for all of you."

"*That's* the understatement of the century."

She could see how upset he was. "Maybe a compromise is in order? What about if you are the driver? You take them and pick them up, and, that way, you can be sure they're going where they should be, and nowhere else. And meet the other kids, too. She is a junior in high school, Caleb. She'll be going off to college soon. And she's a good kid. Slacken up on the rope and see how it goes."

Caleb nodded, a weary smile tugging at the corners of his lips. "Don't remind me about college. But, yeah, you're probably right. Thanks, Taylor."

"Of course I'm right," she said, laughing lightly. "Even if I'm not, you'd better say I am because I'm doing you a big favor today."

"True, true," he replied. "I know it's a long shot, too. It's going to be painstaking to go through our list."

As they drove through town, Taylor couldn't shake the feeling that they were on the wrong trail. She didn't feel like Sullivan had any connection to Lydia. Her gut said no. Still yet, she couldn't dismiss the possibility that he held a grudge.

People could nurse grudges for longer than anyone expected, letting them simmer until they boiled over and made them do something crazy.

They pulled up to a run-down trailer park on the outskirts of town. One that was known for a lot of drug use.

"I see Hart's Trailer Town hasn't changed much since the last time I was here," Caleb said. "Was kind of hoping to see it decimated, with fresh grass growing up in its place to cover all the sins."

He was right. She had nothing against people living in trailers, but this park was a hell hole. Broken-down cars littered the dirt roads, deep potholes were everywhere, and the trailers were in various states of disrepair. It was the kind of place where trouble thrived.

"Yep, I make at least one or two trips out here a week. Mostly nuisance calls. Some fights and trespassing. Child neglect. Lots of angry people here. Stuck in circumstances that some of them were simply born into and can't escape. What's Sullivan's trailer number?"

"16B."

She slowly coasted past a group of kids kicking a ball around. They stopped, and one kid held the ball while they stared, probably wondering who was getting picked up on a warrant. Children who knew more than they should at this age about bad people.

At the next trailer, a woman dressed in a nightshirt sat on a lawn chair, smoking a cigarette, a can of Mountain Dew in her other hand.

She locked eyes with Taylor, shooting daggers at her in a stare down.

Taylor kept going, trying to find anything near to the number they needed. The lots appeared to be numbered by blind monkeys. Not only that, but overgrown foliage was everywhere, covering porches or corners where a number might be. She was glad they were looking in the daylight because she knew from experience the park didn't have streetlights.

"There it is," Caleb said, pointing to a trailer on the left that didn't even look inhabited.

She pulled up and cut the engine, then patted her firearm as reassurance. They got out and Caleb led the way as they approached Sullivan's trailer, then knocked. The front door was weathered and worn and looked like it had been kicked in a few times. Plastic bags on the porch were ripped open and trash was strewn about.

Dirty diapers were in the midst, too. It smelled terribly.

Taylor hated the thought of a baby living there.

The door creaked open, revealing a girl with dirty blonde hair, long and stringy as it hung around her face. She couldn't have been over eighteen and the dark circles under her eyes made her look like a zombie.

"What did we do now?" she asked, her eyes without a single light. Then she turned to look behind her.

Sullivan was standing in the dimly lit interior.

"What the hell do you want?" he grunted, his voice laced with suspicion. "I ain't got no warrants."

"We need to ask you a few questions," Caleb said, his tone authoritative.

Sullivan's gaze flicked between them, his jaw clenched.

"Oh, I know you," he said. "You're that son of a—"

"Yep, that's me. But I'm not here about that," Caleb said, interrupting him mid-sentence.

Taylor braced herself for confrontation, but Sullivan surprised her by stepping aside, allowing them to enter. They didn't step completely into the living room kitchen combo, but the girl and Sullivan went to the couch and plopped down.

There wasn't a baby to be seen. Nor any baby stuff.

Even though they didn't go far into the trailer, Taylor couldn't help but notice the clutter and disarray. Dirty dishes piled in the sink, and a stale odor hung in the air. She'd seen worse but this one was still up there in the top twenty—at least.

"I've checked in with my parole officer and just did a drug test yesterday. I ain't going back," Sullivan said.

Caleb wasted no time getting to the point, questioning Sullivan about his whereabouts from the day Lydia was abducted to the weeks after.

Sullivan leaned back and crossed his ankles, then grinned.

"I'm sure you're expecting me to say I have no idea where I was yesterday, much less a year ago."

Caleb shook his head.

"I have no expectations from you, Sullivan. Just answer the question."

Sullivan nodded to the girl. "Tell 'em, baby."

She looked baffled. "I don't know."

He leaned forward, now angry. "You don't know where we were on November the 10th a year ago? And for at least three days after?"

Suddenly her dead eyes changed, and she nodded.

"Oh, we were at the hospital," she said. "I had a caesarean and then complications. I didn't get to take Jade home until four days later. Daniel stayed by my side the whole time."

Caleb looked at Taylor.

"That's easy to confirm," she said. "Do you have the birth certificate?"

Zombie Girl nodded and went down the narrow hallway. They were all silent until she returned and handed a thick piece of paper to Taylor.

It was a birth certificate and it listed Sullivan as the father.

Taylor handed it back to the girl.

"That checks out but where is the baby now?" Taylor asked. Not that it mattered, but she was curious.

The girl hung her head.

"Where do you think?" Sullivan said, his tone icy. "Dumbass Mommy who can't even remember her own daughter's birthday left her locked in the car when it was hot as hades this summer. Nearly killed her, so now she's in the system and there went our food stamps, too."

"I didn't mean to," the girl said, looking up at Taylor with eyes that swam with tears. "I forgot she was with me, is all. I just forgot."

"Let's go," Caleb said, heading out the door.

Taylor followed. She felt disgusted. She'd bet a dollar the girl was high when she'd done it, too. While a part of her wanted to grab the girl and drag her away from Sullivan and the trailer park —maybe get her on the right track—she knew it wasn't that easy. She didn't look abused ... just sad. And unless she wanted help and came looking for it, she'd boomerang right back as soon as she was out of Taylor's sight.

They got into the car and slowly pulled off, making their way out of the park. Taylor felt like she needed a shower. She also couldn't shake the feeling of disappointment. Sullivan might have had a history with Caleb, but it seemed he wasn't their guy this time. This was going to be a long process. But she'd promised— and she always kept her promises.

She just hoped that once they were at the end of the list, Caleb would accept that Lydia was gone.

"Alright. Where to next?" she asked.

CHAPTER 15

*T*aylor was in the middle of writing a ticket to a seventeen-year-old kid doing fifty-three in a school zone in his jacked-up pickup when the call came over the radio that the warrant was ready and she could go get Wyatt.

Lucky for them, he'd gone right back to work, thinking he was untouchable, but his prints came up all over numerous broken items in Allison's house. A neighbor also claimed to have seen him pull up that night before she went to bed.

Taylor tossed the citation into the boy's truck, letting it flutter onto his lap. "Don't let me catch you speeding again," she said, then turned and went to her patrol car, got in and headed toward the plastics factory on the outskirts of town, her heart pounding with determination.

When she arrived, she drove straight up to the guardhouse that blocked access to the parking lot. A grizzled redneck with a wad of tobacco bulging from his cheek nodded.

"What can I do you for?" he said, smiling and showing off his blackened teeth.

He thought he was funny with his turn of phrase.

"I'm on police business, and I need to know which section of the building I'd find Wyatt Heaton."

The guard's eyes widened in surprise as he spat a glob of tobacco juice onto the ground. "Wyatt? What's he done now? Last time it was for not paying child support," he grumbled, his voice thick with suspicion.

"Please open the gate and point me to the right direction," she said briskly.

He gave her a sarcastic salute and pointed at the north building, then hit the button inside the shack. "Give 'em hell," he called out as she drove through.

Taylor wasted no time in heading in that direction. She parked her cruiser close to the entrance and stormed inside, her boots echoing loudly against the concrete floor.

Approaching a supervisor she didn't recognize, Taylor flashed her badge and wasted no time in stating her purpose. "I have a warrant for the arrest of Wyatt Heaton," she declared, her voice cutting through the noise of the bustling factory floor. "He needs to come with me."

"Oh, shit," the man said. "What for?"

Damn, they were nosy.

"Aggravated stalking, vandalism, and burglary," Taylor snapped, her anger simmering just beneath the surface. "Now, where is he?"

"That sucks for me. Now I'm a man down," he said, pointing toward the farthest door on the other side of the room.

The cacophony of machinery filled the air as Taylor made her way through the maze of equipment, every technician's curious stare following her as she passed. Some of the guys looked nervous, then relieved when she didn't stop at their stations. That didn't stop a couple wolf whistles.

Just as she spotted Wyatt among the workers, he caught sight of her, too, and made a break for it. Taylor chased after him but, just as she reached out to grab his shirt, her foot slipped on an oil spot, sending her crashing to the ground with a resounding thud.

Pain shot through her hip as she struggled to regain her footing, but, by the time she managed to stand, Wyatt was gone.

Cursing under her breath because she'd just made a fool out of herself and lost her suspect, Taylor ignored the pain in her hip and sprinted out to the parking lot, her eyes scanning frantically for any sign of Wyatt's escape.

He was nowhere to be seen.

She ran all the way to the guard shack—doing her best not to limp—and reached it in less than two minutes.

Dumbo was watching her, his mouth agape.

"Which way did he go?" she asked, panting.

"Who? I didn't see anyone." He gazed around as though wondering what he was supposed to be looking for.

She could see right through him. He was lying.

"Do you want to go to jail for obstruction of justice?" She looked at his name tag then back up at his beady eyes. "Junior?"

"I swear—I didn't see him! See, there's his truck right over there," he said, pointing to an older red Tacoma with shiny rims that probably cost more than the whole truck.

"You backwoods idiot," she shot back. "You're covering for him, and you'd better hope I don't see it on a camera."

Frustrated and seething with anger, Taylor radioed for backup, her mind racing with the realization that she needed to find Allison and ensure her safety before Wyatt could track her down.

With a heavy heart, she grabbed her phone to call Allison to see where she thought her train-wreck of a boyfriend would run to hide. Her reputation and bruised ego couldn't afford to let him slip through her fingers again.

CHAPTER 16

lackbird singing in the dead of night … On a bright Sunday afternoon, Lydia was standing at the window, watching Blackbird fly away, hoping he'd lead someone back to rescue her. Blackbirds weren't like pigeons and didn't usually carry messages, but she ignored that reminder and instead clung to the tiny sliver of hope and comfort the bird brought to her.

She'd just finished a chapter in her book earlier that morning on how to set up a survival kitchen to cook rats. She'd shivered to think of it but, on the other hand, if Dom ever left and didn't return, she might have to succumb to catching one of the small mice she'd seen a few times in her room. However, there was no way for her to make fire so it would have to be a sushi-served rat.

Strange things she used to never think about now rambled about in her mind.

The book was at least not totally boring, though the author sounded like he had quite an inflated ego. He rattled on about how awesome he and his ways are. But he had a point about the rats. The chance that someone new to living and hunting outside wasn't going to be bringing down a deer or other big game, at least not for a long while, was valid.

Other than his high opinion of himself that was woven through the page, his information sounded very useful. Lydia had nothing to compare it to, considering she wasn't any type of survivalist. The most she'd ever worried about in an emergency was bread, water, and batteries. And a phone charger.

She read a chapter on how to dispose of a dead body, too, and the page was turned down.

Dom was taking notes.

Sometimes the idea of death beckoned to her like a lost friend. Then she thought of her children and banned the thought to the back of her mind.

Lydia looked at the clouds in the sky. It might rain. She hoped it did because listening to the rain broke up the monotony of the day.

She still remembered how hard it was for her the weeks after Dom brought her to her prison. She'd always been an over-achiever, her thumbs in so many pies that her days swirled by so fast she'd drop into the bed eventually, wondering what had just happened.

Going from that kind of busy life to days filled with nothing but waiting and wishing, fear and dread, made her feel empty and disconnected.

After a few months, though, she'd started to see the involuntary pause in her busy life as an opportunity to reflect. To contemplate how to live her life differently once she was free.

And she would be free one day.

She'd not let herself think anything different.

When she heard the door open at the top of the stairs, she nearly tripped over the chain in her rush to get away from the window. The sudden movement sent pain shrieking from the wound now on her other ankle.

She sat on the mattress quickly.

"Lovely Lydia … it's dinner time," Dom called out as he came down. He sounded like he was in a good mood.

He tossed a brown bag at her, and she caught it mid-air.

The bag was from Panera Bread, a restaurant she was very familiar with. It was Caleb's favorite lunch place when they went to Atlanta. She was nervous to look inside, expecting a trick. The bag probably held a can of beanie wienies.

"Go ahead," he said. "Look."

He pulled a bottle of pills from his pocket and held them up.

"Antibiotics. Take them."

He tossed them to her, and she caught them in mid-air.

Dom sat in the chair and crossed his legs, bringing one ankle up to rest over his knee, a sitting position known to be used by those who wanted to appear confident and dominant.

Lydia opened the bag and peeked in. She tried to keep her expression under control but, surely, he saw her eyes widen.

Salad.

He could probably hear her pulse quicken from where he sat. Her mouth watered with anticipation, but she carefully folded the top of the bag back down and set it aside. She wanted that salad so badly, but she wanted to enjoy it alone, not with him staring at her.

"So, you want to eat it later," he said, grinning like a Cheshire cat. "I'll allow it. We need to get you stronger."

Of course, he wasn't getting her something fresh to eat out of the kindness of his heart. Every move he made was calculated. Why did he want her stronger?

When the smile left his face, he stared at her blankly.

"Church was boring today, thanks for asking. I've been approached about becoming a deacon. They really like me there. I'm able to stand in for the Sunday School teacher when he's out. My knowledge of the Bible far surpasses anyone else in our class. But you know what I don't like, Lydia?"

She blinked. His arrogance was sickening. Of course they liked him there. One of the most widely known traits of a psychopath was superficial charm. Most fell for it as long as they weren't brought into the inner circle of relationships where cracks begin to show until everything breaks wide open, and their true colors are discovered.

"I don't like that they sugarcoat the Bible. The lessons are so watered down these days, and hardly ever do they discuss the good stuff. If I had the choice, I'd focus on teaching what others are hiding. Take Judges 19, for example. I do have to say, it's a fantastic read. Some refer to it as a *Text of Terror*—those parts of the good book that are full of the real juicy stuff like rape and murder. Even sex trafficking and pointing out the proper place of a woman, straight from the words of God."

Lydia didn't know the Bible that well, and she dreaded where Dom was headed.

He looked almost giddy as he continued. "Look at you, Lydia. You are, in a sense, my concubine. Did you know that God approved of men taking concubines! He approved of men doing what they pleased with them, too, even if it meant murder."

She tried not to flinch visibly.

He smiled in a pitying way at her obvious discomfort. "In Judges 19, a Levite and his concubine seek refuge in Gibeah, only to be met with hostility. The men of the city demand to rape the Levite, but the host offers his virgin daughter and the concubine instead." Dom paused, letting the weight of the passage sink in before continuing. "The concubine is handed over to the mob, subjected to unspeakable horrors throughout the night. In the morning, she is left for dead at the doorstep. She's eventually dismembered by the Levite with her body parts being scattered in twelve parts to symbolize the sins of the Gibeahites. But he neglects to tell his fellow Israelites that he himself sent his concubine out to those men as his replacement, because they wanted him first."

Lydia could see why the church didn't dwell on that chapter. If Dom wasn't making it up, the brutality of such a story would make readers confront the darkness of evil and misogyny that began way back in the beginning, and not just with Eve.

"What do you think of that?" he asked.

She looked at him, not blinking.

"Sadly, I have some long meetings tomorrow and need to leave too early to see you in the morning. I also might be late coming home. Perhaps the salad will hold you over."

Please don't take it away. Please don't take it away.

"I bet you wonder about me all day, don't you, Lydia?"

She didn't wonder so much as sometimes hope he got hit by a truck. Then other times she worried that he would, and she'd die chained in his basement, forgotten by the world.

"You probably wonder if I'm in a relationship. I'm not. At least not currently. I was married before, though," he said. "Not once, but twice. Obviously, it didn't work out. Oh, and we can't let the church know about my little matrimonial detours. Of course, they don't want a deacon who has been married and divorced. Must keep this good-guy reputation going, don't we?"

Dom as a good guy or a husband was too hard to imagine.

As a father would be even harder to visualize. Lydia hoped he hadn't spawned any children. For their sake, at least.

"My wives never could understand that they weren't my priority. I like my alone time. Even when I was a kid, I'd hike for hours and hours, alone. I quite enjoy my own company, if you can believe that."

Oh, she could believe it.

"I have to admit, the sound of a female nagging me can send me into a murderous rage."

She wondered if that meant he'd done away with his past partners.

He stood and stretched.

"I'll leave you now, dear. While I'm away I want you to think about Judges 19. Ponder on what you think that your God would have me do with you. Offer you up to others, or, well—you know, the other alternative. Chop, chop."

She felt a tingle run up her spine and make the hairs on her neck stand up. He'd never alluded to an ending between them before.

Sex slaves were known to be passed around in the black market. Sold to the highest bidder when each master tired of them. Was Dom involved in that kind of circuit? Lydia couldn't imagine he would be, as that would be taking chances with his privacy, and he seemed too smart for that.

His hint about doing away with her like the man in the Bible had done with his concubine would make more sense, if she was predicting how he'd get her out of his life.

She realized she was holding her breath, her body tight and every muscle tensed. She let it go slowly. Dom probably only wanted to scare her, but his twisting of the Bible wasn't going to work.

God gave men free will. It said that in the Bible, too, she knew that much. He didn't send Dom to abduct her or guide him to torture her. There would be justice for every person who committed such heinous acts. If Dom acted on his threats, she would be gone but, eventually, he'd pay for it.

Good would triumph over evil.

Not to mention that God— and Blackbird— was the only thing keeping her hanging on. She would not let Dom soil it for her and she'd think of God as only gentle and good, and she found solace in His mercy and compassion. She fully believed that somehow, someday, He would show her the way home.

CHAPTER 17

*T*aylor drove in silence for a while longer, the rhythm of the road lulling her into a sense of quiet contemplation, the only noise the excited sound of Diesel's panting from the backseat. Her mind was on Allison. A full week had gone by since the excitement about Wyatt Heaton, and no one had seen or heard a peep from him.

He was hiding well.

Allison was lying low, too, but she was nervous. Not only about Heaton, but about where she and the kids were going to live. Mabel was checking into some resources, but until they found Heaton, Taylor didn't want them going anywhere.

The department had put out an all-points bulletin to all the surrounding counties, and she'd checked every one of Heaton's family members' properties that Allison could think to send her to.

As was common in the south, everyone's lips were sealed about their wanted kinfolk. Some of them even said that Allison had it coming, for filing against Wyatt for the domestic abuse. Now she had more than just her boyfriend wanting harm to come to her.

Heaton's redneck father claimed that a man had a right to keep his significant other in line. It had taken everything in Taylor to walk away from his porch without catching an assault and battery charge herself.

At the department, she'd taken a lot of heat for letting Heaton get away from her. The only ones who hadn't given her any shit about it were Penner and the sheriff.

Shane thought it was a hilarious story until she'd walked out of his office and wouldn't speak to him for two days running. She hoped she'd be the one to bring Heaton in, but he'd better hope she wasn't.

Because things were at a bit of a standstill with that, and they'd reached the end of their list without any leads, she'd agreed to go to Amicalola Falls with Caleb.

As they neared the area, she felt a mixture of sadness and adrenaline coursing through her veins. This was familiar territory, a place where she'd spent countless hours combing through the dense undergrowth in search of clues. A place she still went to on her own when she could squeeze out the time. On her own with Diesel, that is.

"I can't believe we didn't find a single lead with that list of names," Caleb said, pounding his fist on his armrest.

Diesel stopped panting, suddenly alert at the change in energy.

"That just tells us that we need to continue to focus our energy on finding her remains somewhere in here," Taylor said softly. "The sheriff won't finance any more searches, but that doesn't mean we can't."

That wasn't what he wanted to hear, but it was what he *needed* to hear. She had to keep him from false hope that Lydia was alive, especially now that they'd exhausted the list of his arrestees who might've been holding a grudge. Caleb had pulled up all of those who had done time because of his arrest, and all those who had left a memory of being overly vindictive toward him. It was a long list with at least three dozen names, but the ones they hadn't visited they'd been able to track down online and cross off the list, until they were down to none.

Parking the car at the trailhead, Taylor was out first, then Diesel, and she waited on Caleb to send one of the girls a quick reply to their text before he got out.

They set out quietly, their footsteps echoing in the stillness of the forest as Diesel ran ahead. He'd go about fifty feet, then turn and see if they followed, and backtrack when they turned a different way. He wouldn't let Taylor out of his sight for more than a few seconds.

It was a nice day, and the air was thick with the scent of pine needles and damp earth, the sound of rushing water in the distance a perfect soundtrack to their hike.

"Want to take a different route?" Taylor asked, casting a glance at Caleb.

He shook his head, his brow furrowed in concentration. "Not really," he admitted. "We've covered so much ground here already, I'm not sure where else to look."

"Well, let's just keep moving," she said.

They pressed on, looking once again for any evidence that had been passed over from all their manpower and searches. Beneath the surface beauty of the forest lay a deeper, more somber truth and Taylor felt heavy with sadness.

Diesel galloped along, his joy at being free in nature showing with every bounce. He sniffed a dozen or more spots, his tail twitching with curiosity over what critter had come before him.

The contrast between his happiness and their discouraged energy was jolting. This was the place where Lydia had vanished without a trace, leaving behind only unanswered questions and lingering grief. Every rustle of the leaves, every whisper of the wind seemed to echo with the pain of her absence, more so for Caleb than her, she was sure. But she could feel it, too.

"Was Sam mad that you're using more of your time off to help me?" Caleb asked, breaking the silence.

She hesitated. "I don't think "mad" is the right word. He's concerned, I guess you could say. He thinks that this isn't helpful to your mental health."

Caleb didn't respond.

"He reminded me that you made me a promise," she added.

"I know. And I am going to let it go. I'm just not ready. Give me a little more time, Taylor."

"You got it." How could she say no?

Caleb was an emotional wreck. His life was, too.

Taylor was worried about him.

Two hours passed in a blur of sweat and exhaustion, the sun sinking lower on the horizon with each passing minute.

When Diesel saw a blackbird ahead on the trail, standing and staring at them from the ground in front of a tree, he barked, startling both Taylor and Caleb, then he charged playfully.

The bird flew off just before Diesel got to it.

Taylor spotted something glinting from where he began to dig at the underbrush, where the blackbird had been. With a surge of excitement, she hurried forward.

"Move over, Diesel," she said, pushing aside the thick foliage to where the glint led her to an earring. It was a stud style in the shape of a heart, white with a gold border. No backing on it.

She slipped on a plastic glove from her pocket and picked it up.

"Caleb, look!" she exclaimed, holding it up, her heart pounding with anticipation.

He rushed over to join her, his eyes widening in disbelief as he took in the sight before him. "Could this be …?"

Taylor nodded, her pulse quickening with excitement. "It's possible," she said, her voice barely above a whisper. "Did Lydia ever have earrings like this one?"

He studied it briefly, then nodded. "I really think this is from the set I got her on our first anniversary. I know they were hearts. When we get to a signal, I'll look on my phone. I'm sure I have a photo from that day."

"We need to get it back to the lab for analysis. It might have her DNA." She secured the earring in the glove and knotted it up and put it in her pocket.

"Good boy, Diesel!" She said a silent thanks to the bird, too, before they started back down the trail.

Her energy was renewed, and they made good time back to the truck.

As they drove back to town, she couldn't help but let a glimmer of hope stir within. If it was Lydia's earring, that proved that she was indeed in that forest at some point. Maybe, just maybe, they were finally closing in on finding closure.

But they'd chased after so many false leads and dead ends. And until they had concrete proof in hand, she knew they couldn't afford to let their guard down.

"Caleb, you have to consider that it might not be hers," Taylor said. "There are a lot of hikers on this trail. I don't want you to get too excited, just to be let down again. And, if it is hers, that confirms the story that she was left out here."

"Maybe. Maybe not. I won't pin too much on it. I swear."

But he would. She knew that.

CHAPTER 18

*L*ydia peeked out the window, and the squirrel she was watching froze, then turned and looked her right in the eye. She'd watched a lot of squirrels over the last months, but this one was new. Strangely, it didn't have a tail. Lydia was sure that squirrels needed their tail for many reasons, especially for balance in all the acrobatics they did daily.

Probably even for warmth.

Didn't they wrap their tails around their bodies in the winter?

She would think that the little guy's coordination would be compromised, let alone body temperature.

Whether it wasn't born with a tail or had lost it to a predator, she wasn't sure, but it was alarming. After it decided she wasn't a threat, it scampered over to the window, peering at her closer. It tilted its head, looking curious as it gazed at her.

She smiled back at it.

Then the squirrel took off and ran up a tree, just as fast as any other squirrel she'd seen do the same thing. It was as though he was trying to show her that she didn't have anything to worry about.

"Your name is now Digby," Lydia whispered. "Please come back to visit."

Little Digby was her lesson for the day. If he could survive and even thrive through his adversity, then she could, too.

Right on cue, she heard the door at the top of the stairs fly open.

Dom stormed down and into the dimly-lit room, his face contorted with fury as he paced back and forth like a caged animal. "Can you believe the nerve of that woman?" he bellowed, his voice echoing off the walls. "Rachel had the audacity to challenge me in front of the entire staff today!"

Lydia's heart sank as she braced herself for another one of Dom's explosive rants. She kept her gaze fixed on the floor, silently praying for the strength to endure his tirade.

Rachel was his nemesis and he'd ranted about her before.

Lydia had struggled all morning, before the squirrel encounter. She'd made the mistake of having allowed herself to think of things she usually pushed away. She'd held Zoey, wetting the doll with hours of tears as she thought of all her daughters, worried that they had already forgotten her.

"I am the lead attorney, the top dog, and that little bitch had the gall to question my authority," Dom continued, his voice dripping with venom. "She thinks she knows better than me. Thinks she can undermine my decisions!"

As Dom's anger reached a fever pitch, Lydia felt a knot form in her stomach. She knew better than to interrupt or offer any semblance of resistance. All she could do was listen in silence, her mind racing with a mix of fear and desperation.

"Oh, but you'd better believe that I put her in her place. I made it clear who's in charge around there," Dom boasted, his chest puffed out with self-importance. "But mark my words, Lydia, I won't let her challenge me like that again."

Lydia wished that she could warn Rachel that she was now on Dom's target list.

He paced, his face a mask of anger. Then he stopped and looked at the ceiling, and breathed deeply, appearing to try to calm himself.

"She pretended to want to be my friend when she first came to work there," he said, turning to Lydia. "I allowed it but what I wanted to tell her was that friendships are pointless. Relationships without sex always turn out to be pointless, burdensome, and not to mention boring. I kept her around though just in case she might become useful. Look at you, Lydia; I guess you could say we're friends, yes?"

She stared at him, emotionless.

"ANSWER ME!" he bellowed, his face going mottled with rage.

Other than her pulse pounding so loud in her ears that he must be able to hear it, too, Lydia said nothing.

"You're right. We're not friends. This relationship is purely transactional. When you stop giving me what I need, it will be over," he said, bringing his voice down.

He sat in the wooden chair and kicked off his dress shoes, then glared at her.

"Rub my feet."

Lydia rose from her mattress and, shaking, she went to him, sinking onto the rug as she immediately picked up a foot and began massaging it. Sometimes a foot massage was enough for him, and it would relax him enough to go upstairs and go to bed.

Other times, he'd go up and turn the music on, then return to the basement.

What would happen next would be horrific. It always came after the music.

Squeezing, biting, and probably even choking.

She rubbed his foot even harder and prayed silently with all her might.

CHAPTER 19

*a*llison's heart pounded like a drum as she was abruptly awoken by Mabel's urgent voice, piercing through the veil of sleep. "Get to the safe room, now!" Mabel's tone tolerated no argument, and Allison's terror spurred her into action.

She jumped up from the bed and went to Chelsea.

"What's going on?" Allison asked as she peeled the cover from her dozing little girl.

"No time to talk. I'll get Toby and meet you down there. Don't stop to grab anything. Just get Chelsea and go!"

With trembling hands, Allison guided Chelsea out of the bed, then picked her up in her arms. Chelsea wrapped her arms and legs around her, snuggling into her neck.

Mabel was only a few steps ahead of her, but she stopped at another room, her usually gentle voice bellowing for others to wake up.

Within just a couple of minutes, everyone from the house was ushered into the cramped space under the stairs. Mabel did a quick headcount, handed Toby off to another woman, then bolted the door and secured it with a board across it.

They were only in complete darkness for a few seconds

before Mabel had a camping light on, casting eerie shadows against the walls.

"Someone has set off the alarm at the gate," Mabel said. "County is on its way to check it out."

The air felt heavy with fear as they huddled together, the small room barely accommodating their group. Allison had been told about the safe room, but this was her first time seeing it. Other than two crib-sized mattresses set on wooden platforms against the wall, the dim lighting revealed that the narrow passageway also included metal shelving at the back, stocked with survival supplies like candles, canned goods, and utensils.

Her gaze lingered on the boxed ammunition, but she didn't see any guns.

She lowered Chelsea to the mattress, then realized her daughter was now awake, her eyes wide and her face pale in the shadows.

"Mommy, where are we?"

"It's okay, sweetie. We're just having a bedtime adventure. See, Miss Mabel is here, too."

As Toby's cries echoed in the cramped space, Allison's heart constricted with fear.

"Here, let me have him," she said, taking him from the girl who roomed across the hall from them. She rocked him gently, and, beside her, Chelsea trembled with fear, her wide eyes darting around the confined space.

Toby fell back asleep against her chest, Allison holding him tighter than usual.

Mabel's soothing voice broke through the silence. "I'm sure it's not going to be needed, but we have firearms in the cabinets beneath these mattresses. Only grab one if you know how to use it; otherwise, if it comes to that, you huddle at the back with the kids and let those who know how to handle a weapon move to the front."

Allison's mind raced with questions, her fear threatening to overwhelm her. "When can we go out?" she asked, her voice barely above a whisper.

Mabel's response was swift and unwavering. "When the police have secured the area inside and out," she said, her tone leaving no room for argument.

As they waited in tense silence, the women exchanged quiet murmurs, their voices filled with fear and uncertainty. One woman shared a harrowing tale of her own safe room she used to have, telling how high tech it was but also how useless, since the one she needed to be safe from knew it was there and how to get in.

"Who do you think is out there?" Denise asked. "I hope it's not Jeff. I swear, though, I haven't told anyone where we are. My mom doesn't even have this address."

"I should hope not," Mabel said. "Even the closest relative can be harassed to the point of giving us up. It's imperative that no one knows where we are. Not only for your personal safety—and your loved ones on the outside—but we must especially think of the children."

Allison's thoughts swirled with fear and suspicion, her mind racing with the possibility of betrayal. Could one of the women's partners be responsible for the trespass? Did one of them slip up and reveal the location of The Lighthouse?

It couldn't be Wyatt. He didn't know where they were. No one did, other than Taylor. Anyway, Wyatt was still on the run. She'd heard that he lost his job, and, as soon as they found him, he was going to be sitting in jail on enough charges to keep him there for a while. He was going to have a felony on his record. That meant he'd never be able to get to his dream job as a firefighter. Not in Georgia, anyway.

Allison couldn't even imagine how angry he was at her now.

Amber, Chelsea's new friend, came and sat down next to them.

Like some kind of magician, Mabel pulled a children's book

and two flashlights from somewhere and handed them over along with two small, but furry, teddy bears.

The girls scooted closer to sit against the wall and Amber held the book while Chelsea turned pages, each holding a flashlight in one hand and the teddy bears in their laps.

Finally, after what felt like an eternity, the seven knocks signaled their salvation. Relief washed over Allison as Deputy Kuno announced they were safe and could come out.

Mabel went out first, looked around, then beckoned for the rest of them to join her.

"We've cleared the property," Grimes said. "Penner and Gray are still out there, going over it one more time to be sure. Deputy Kuno and I have already searched inside three times, and no one is here."

"Thank God," Mabel said.

Allison could see her physically relax with relief.

"Oh, well. Can't sleep now," Denise said. "I'll make coffee if anyone is interested. And hot chocolate in case the kids want it."

Both Amber and Chelsea were happy about that and followed Denise. The rest of them found spots around the living room.

Allison had to agree. Sleeping was out of the question. Her nerves still thrummed with tension. The offer of coffee and hot chocolate provided a semblance of normalcy, but her mind remained clouded with worry.

"Gray will give you the report of the exterior search," Grimes said.

Penner and Gray arrived amidst the chaos. Allison's heart skipped a beat at the sight of Taylor's familiar face, her presence an immediate source of comfort.

Taylor was all business as she stood in the doorway, her hand resting on her hip holster. "We found footprints on both sides of the gate, leading to the porch and then around the house," she said. "Looks like someone was searching for an unlocked window. No strange vehicle tire tracks, so we think they were on foot. Possibly parked a few miles from here, somewhere unseen."

"Won't find unlocked windows here," Mabel said. "But let's go see who it was. I'm sure the camera had to have caught them at some point."

Grimes, Kuno, and Penner said their goodbyes after Taylor said she'd finish up and write it up, and they promised to do a few more runs up and down the road to search for anyone out and about.

Mabel led Taylor to her bedroom.

Allison trailed behind them, Toby still sleeping on her shoulder.

Mabel's room was nearly as big as the living area of the house. Her bed was in the middle, with an office area alcove on one side, and a small TV area on the other. The walls were adorned with more than thirty framed photographs, all of them holding photos of different women, some of them posing with children.

Mabel noticed Allison's gaze lingering on the photos, her voice soft with pride as she explained their significance. "Those are the ones who passed through here and managed to build a new life. Ones that felt safe from the hands of the men who abused them," she said, her eyes flickering with emotion. "This wall reminds me to keep going, even when I feel exhausted and tired of it all, like tonight."

Allison looked at the smiling faces in the photographs, feeling a connection with them in some small way. Despite the hardships they had faced, there was a sense of peace in their smiles, a reminder that there was light at the end of the tunnel.

She would make it, too.

"You were already up?" Taylor asked Mabel, seeing the television running.

"I sure was. I think my intuition has been nudging me all day. I just couldn't settle it. Thank goodness, because that gave me some extra time to get everyone downstairs. Hold on, it's ready to go." She clicked the button on her monitor and the footage started up.

Allison went to the couch. Her neck was aching from holding Toby. She should go put him in his bed, but, as long as Taylor was there, she wanted to be near her. They'd been having a lot of phone conversation lately, as Allison tried to come up with places to look for Wyatt. Taylor was fast becoming a good friend and one of the only people that Allison felt she could truly trust.

Other than Mabel, of course. That woman would give her life for a stranger.

Toby started to wake, and Allison moved over to the rocking chair and concentrated on rocking him back to sleep. He was going to be in a terrible mood in the morning if he didn't get his sleep.

On the news, an anchorwoman stood in front of a house, and a red banner was moving across the screen, an Amber Alert for a missing child.

Allison held Toby closer, thankful that she'd been able to keep her kids safe throughout the sudden drama of her life.

"That's Heaton," Taylor said from behind her.

Allison had the weirdest sensation flutter over her. She stood and went to the monitor, looking between Taylor and Mabel at the screen.

In the footage that Mabel had frozen, she saw Wyatt climbing over the fence, the moonlight catching him just right and giving her a good look at his face.

"I can't believe it," she mumbled, feeling like she was in shock. "I swear, I didn't—"

She felt her knees going weak and thrust Toby toward Taylor, who caught him with one arm and her with the other.

Mabel helped and they both led her to the couch.

"Of course you didn't mean to," Mabel said. "But have you told anyone our location? A friend? Maybe your mother?"

"No, I haven't."

"He figured it out somehow," Taylor said. "That means you can't stay here, Allison. He'll be back, I have no doubt about that. We can't take the chance that he'll gain access inside before we get to the safe room or before help comes."

Panic surged through Allison, her mind reeling with the implications of Wyatt's return.

"I ... I," she stammered. "I'm so sorry, Mabel ..."

"We'll figure it out," Mabel said, rubbing her back in soothing circles.

Allison wasn't so sure. She didn't have a wide network of people like most people did. Where would they go? Her eyes traveled back to the television, the banner going across the screen with details of the child that had been stolen right out of her bed. The mother desperate to have her back.

Was Wyatt coming for Toby? Or for her?

He had never even changed Toby's diapers or learned the first thing about how to fix up a bottle of formula.

She felt nausea set in as she imagined Toby declining under his father's care.

"Oh no," Mabel said, her attention going to the television where Allison was looking. "I know them. That's Gwen and her daughter, Jill," Mabel said, pointing to a photograph on the wall behind them. "They were here a few years ago, can't remember exactly when."

Taylor sat down next to Allison, still holding Toby as they listened to the news bulletin. A woman stepped up to the mike, looking drawn and exhausted. She ran her hands through her hair and swallowed hard.

"Please, if you have my daughter, bring her home. No questions asked, just leave her back at her grandfather's house unharmed. Please. Also, Jill has asthma. She always needs her medication near her and, and ..." she stopped, bursting into tears.

An elderly woman stepped into view and led her away.

The reporter took her place. "As we've said, eight-year-old Jill

Kelley was last seen when she went to bed at her grandfather's house in Birmingham, Alabama, around ten o'clock this evening. Her grandfather heard a noise around midnight and went to check on Jill and found her room empty and showing evidence of a scuffle. A search is being conducted of the property and surrounding areas as we speak. Please report any tips or sightings of Jill Kelley at the number below."

Mabel shook her head. "That woman can't catch a break."

"I don't recognize her," Taylor replied. "You said she was here once?"

"She was, but they were out-of-towners so you wouldn't know her. She and her husband were renting a house on the lake for the weekend when he assaulted her. The daughter was asleep, thankfully, but the neighbors heard her cries and called the police. Gwen wouldn't press charges. I got her here for the night and, after she showed me photos of what she'd been through the last few years, I got Pam Kleiser over here. Pam made her see that she needed to get away, not only for her sake, but for her child. They were moved to another network that helped Gwen start over. The dad tried to win custody but ended up losing all parental rights, so I'm not at all surprised to see this happening."

"You really think he took her?" Allison asked. Her heart broke for the inconsolable mother. There couldn't be anything worse than not knowing where your child was.

"Well, I don't know, but he was a smart one. Cunning, too. Like a fox. They were a wealthy couple, but Gwen walked away with nearly none of the marital assets, just to get it all over with and get him out of her life."

Allison could relate, though she really didn't have anything of value. What she did have was now either burnt or in pieces. She thought of her grandmother's rocking chair.

"That's tragic," Taylor said. "I hope they find the girl, but, Allison, we need to talk about you and your children. We must make a plan but, in the meantime, I want you to pack up. You're all coming out to my farm, and we'll keep you safe while we figure this out."

Allison couldn't say thank you because her throat immediately filled with tears. She couldn't describe the relief that fell over her.

Mabel was amazing but Allison no longer felt safe under her roof. Not for her and her kids, and not for the others who lived there, innocent people who could become collateral damage in Wyatt's rampage.

CHAPTER 20

*T*aylor laughed and tried to shield her face when Sam sidled up beside her and used his paddle to slap the water, splashing her as he took off again. Alice was catching up to them, and hopefully would help get Sam back.

"C'mon, Alice," she shouted, "Let's get him!"

Hearing the giggles come out of the usually serious Alice Stone put a huge smile on Taylor's face. She had to admit, with the sun out and gliding across the smooth surface of the lake, it felt good to have a moment away from work. Especially with her two most favorite people in the world. And her dog, Diesel.

Cate had urged her to say yes to Sam and Alice and go out with the kayaks, saying she needed some vitamin D. Taylor had a feeling that Cate was doing what moms do. Especially since Taylor had caught the look of gratitude that Sam had given her mom.

Taylor knew she was a workaholic. But, really, it wasn't even that.

Beneath her tough exterior, she felt responsible to help everyone around her, and she didn't know how to say no. She didn't *want* to say no.

Ever. And that was a problem.

Sam had told her as much the night before when she'd brought Allison and her kids back to the farm with her. He'd kept his worry to himself, though, and Allison didn't suspect that he was anything but welcoming.

Down deep, she wondered if this obsession of hers to fix everything stemmed from her childhood, and how she wished that she would've had more people step in to help her and her sisters. Maybe in all the roles she took on as an adult, she was being to others what she'd needed the most herself.

If she was still going to therapy—*which she wasn't*—she'd probably tell her therapist that she'd had an epiphany.

Now what could she do about it?

That was the million-dollar question.

However, today wasn't the day to ponder it because she wanted to give Sam and Alice the attention they were so obviously starving for. The two of them spent a lot of time together, and, lately, Taylor was rarely a part of it.

Allison was invited to join them on the kayaks, but she'd declined, saying she didn't feel well. Taylor had a feeling the girl didn't want to let Anna watch her kids. Not because she didn't trust Anna but, because the scare they'd had at The Lighthouse was still with her, Allison didn't want them out of her sight.

She was also going to call her mom and ask if there were any distant relatives who would take them in for a short while, at least until Wyatt was found.

Taylor didn't have a lot of hope that Allison's mother would be too helpful, just based on a few things Allison had said about her, but it was worth a try.

She watched Sam move through the water, his biceps bulging with each stroke as he put a lot of distance between them. Diesel turned back and looked at her, a gleam in his eyes. He loved the platform that Sam had made for the kayak, letting him ride in the back, the wind rustling through his hair.

Soon he would make a jump for it, and try to keep up with Sam, swimming to his right.

There was nothing Diesel liked better than to be in the water. Well, except for riding in the truck. That probably took first place in his list of things-dogs-love-to-do.

Taylor laid her paddle across her lap and coasted to a stop just as Alice sidled up next to her and grabbed her kayak to keep them together.

"Dad's showing off," she said, grinning.

"Yep. Boys will be boys," Taylor said. "Let's just rest for a minute. Why don't you tell me what's been going on with you lately. I feel like we hardly get to talk anymore."

Alice laid her paddle down, too.

"Well, that's true because you're gone all the time."

That was something that Taylor loved about Alice. She never beat around the bush. She was always diplomatic, speaking without malice, but she got to the point without a bunch of fluff. She was an old soul.

"I know. I'm sorry," Taylor said. "I promise, I'm going to try harder to be at home more."

Alice looked doubtful. "I really think you should. Dad gets lonely, and it's the kind of lonely that I can only do so much about. He misses you, Taylor. I think he won't tell you how much, but he's always watching the windows when it's late. Waiting and worrying."

That felt like a sucker punch to the gut. And Alice sounded like an adult, not a fourteen-year-old.

"Ouch. But, yeah—I get it."

Alice looked sympathetic. "I'm just telling you what he won't. Not trying to upset you."

"I know. And you're right."

She *was* right, but Sam knew what he was getting into when he asked to marry a cop. She would never have a regular schedule, especially because the sheriff was trusting her more and more with being Shane's sidekick. How could she turn down investigative work when it's what she wanted to do someday, full time? She didn't want to go back to full-time patrol and all the other mundane duties she'd done before. What she wanted was to be named as a detective.

Sam knew that.

Taylor heard a huge splash and saw that, up ahead, Diesel jumped off the kayak and was headed her way. He was probably concerned that she and Alice had stopped.

Sam turned his kayak and waved.

"Enough about your dad," Taylor said. "I want to hear about you. Anything new going on at school?"

She shrugged. "Not really, I guess."

Such a teenage answer. Alice's inner adult was suddenly subdued.

"What about the homecoming dance? Have you decided if you're going or not?"

"I don't know," Alice said, suddenly shy. "It depends if I get done with my presentation for psychology class."

That was so Alice. She was probably the only teenage girl in the state of Georgia who would put a school assignment before something like Homecoming. One of these days, Alice and her strong work ethic were going to blow the socks off a career.

"Okay, so what's it about?" Taylor asked.

Sam started to paddle back to them.

"Social media and its effects on teens. My teacher said that if it's good enough, the principal is going to send an invitation out to all parents and use it for a community awareness assembly."

"Wow. That would be great for you," Taylor said. "She must think you've got the talent to put together a great presentation."

"I guess," Alice said. "I have a long way to go. Right now, I'm still gathering research. Did you know that last year there was a landmark report that found teenagers between ages thirteen and eighteen use an average of nine hours of entertainment media a day, and tweens ages eight to twelve use an average of six hours a day, and that's not including time spent using media for school or homework."

Taylor whistled, shaking her head. She knew that kids and their phones were becoming a huge problem, especially when it came to bullying on social media, but she didn't know the addiction was that bad. "I hope you don't spend that much time on it," she said, giving Alice a serious look.

"Me? No way. I tend to try to find ways for my brain *not* to turn to mush."

They laughed.

"Another statistic," Alice said. "Thirteen-year-olds check their social media more than one hundred times a day."

"That's insane. I bet most parents have no idea," Taylor said. "I think that phones and tablets have become a babysitter in a way, giving moms and dads quiet time while their kids have their noses buried on the internet. It's scary."

If she ever had a kid of her own, she planned to keep them away from social media as long as possible. Maybe even until they went to college. Of course, that probably wasn't feasible, but she could always hope.

"Right, and there are a lot of sick people out there," Alice said. "Did you hear about that eight-year-old girl who went missing from her grandparent's home in Alabama? I bet she was talking to someone on the internet. Probably thought it was a boy her age, and instead met up with some thirty-year-old sicko."

"Yeah, I saw that. I hope they find her." Taylor thought of the news flash she'd seen last night on the television in Mabel's room. It was quite coincidental that the mother and the girl had once stayed there in that very house.

Sam slid between them just as Diesel arrived and tried to climb into Alice's kayak.

"No, Diesel. Go with Dad," she shrieked, pushing his wet body away. "You stink."

"Guess who gets to give him a bath?" Sam said, winking at Alice. "You're the one who insisted he come. Right, Taylor?"

Taylor was lost in thought.

"Um ... Taylor? Earth to Taylor ..." Sam said.

"Oh, yeah. Sorry. What did you say?"

Alice laughed. "Hello, space cadet," she said. "What were you thinking about?"

"I was thinking about how I'm going to smoke you both getting back to the dock," Taylor lied, and took off, paddling as fast and hard as she could.

She had a phone call to make. What if the officer who had written the report of Gwen Kelley's abuse that night she came to The Lighthouse, was none other than Caleb Grimes? And what if because of Gwen coming to the shelter, and deciding then and there not to go back to her marriage, it had set off the husband?

If all that was true, it would mean there was one more person to add to Caleb's list of those who might have a vendetta against him.

That meant that Taylor needed to get Caleb on the phone stat, and meant she needed to beat Alice and Sam by a mile, so that she could squeeze in a phone call without them noticing she was once again working on her day off. She ignored the throbbing in her hip and dug her oar deeper into the water.

$\mathcal{C}$aleb stood at the door, his heart pounding with a mixture of relief and disbelief as Deputy Penner stood aside and allowed Grace to pass by him on her way into the house. It was nearly two o'clock in the morning and he'd thought all his daughters were in bed asleep.

He'd come in after they'd gone up but had checked to make sure they were all safe before he'd gone to bed himself. It took him more than two hours to fall asleep, due to his mind reeling over the discovery that they had one more important lead to follow for Lydia's case. He'd found the photo of them on their anniversary. The earring was a match to those that Lydia had worn that night.

Now he rubbed at his eyes, trying to process what was happening.

"What is going on?" Caleb asked Grace.

She went on to the kitchen, ignoring him.

"Penner, what the hell?" Caleb said.

"Got a noise complaint and went to check it out. House on Pendergrass Street was having a party and packed with under-aged kids."

Caleb shook his head, unable to form a reply. He was embarrassed. Grace was in so much trouble.

"But she wasn't drinking, that I could tell," Penner continued. "She was just headed to her car—I mean, your car. She and her friend, who was highly intoxicated and underage. I've already dropped the other girl off at her house and talked to the parents. I let Grace drive your car home, but I followed close behind."

"Did you write anything up on it?" Caleb asked.

"No. Of course not."

"Thanks, Penner. I'll take it from here." He shut the door and breathed deeply after watching Penner walk toward his car, trying to calm himself down before confronting Grace. He could hear her in the kitchen, and he went there and sat on a bar stool.

She was at the counter, making a smoothie, of all things. Zuri jumped up there and Grace shooed her down.

"Kind of late for snacking," he said, starting off easy.

"I'm up, might as well make it." She hit the button on the blender, drowning out his next question.

He could tell that she knew she was in a lot of trouble, but he had to give her props for not running straight up to her room to hide from the confrontation. She was a tough one.

"Grace," he started when she'd finished with the blender and was pouring up her pink substance. "What were you thinking? Stealing my car to go to a party? A party with underage drinking? You know better."

She brought her smoothie to the counter he sat at, and she stood opposite him, putting a barrier between them as she sipped it. When she set it down, she was calm.

"Dad, I didn't steal the car. I borrowed it."

"You don't have a license to drive after dark. I didn't give you permission to take it. That's stealing, Grace."

"I don't have my license because you are being too protective, and I planned to bring the car back unharmed. That's borrowing."

They stared at each other in a face off.

"To a party. With alcohol." He stated coldly. "Probably older boys, too."

Grace's cheeks flushed with anger, her voice rising as she spoke. "You have to hear me out, Dad! Technically, I wasn't at the party with the other kids. I only went there to pick up Natalie. She called me and said she'd had too much to drink and needed a way home. I wasn't about to let some random guy get her in his car and take advantage of her."

He had to give her props for that.

"I knew that I didn't like the sound of this Natalie James," he said. "Drunk at her age? What's going to happen when she goes off to college and has no rules? She'll end up dead in a week."

"That's a bit dramatic," Grace said. "This isn't about Natalie being drunk. It's about me being a responsible friend. And I know Penner told you that I wasn't drinking. What do you want? A field sobriety test?"

Caleb's jaw tightened. "You should've woken me. I would've gone over there with you."

Grace's eyes welled with tears, her voice shaking. "I don't believe you. In the rare times that you *are* here, it's only in body, not mind and spirit. You're too caught up in your own pain to be of any help to me or Ella. Or even Zoey. We all know that we are just a burden to you now that Mom is gone."

He felt a pang of guilt as Grace's words hit home. He *had* been neglecting his duties as a father, consumed by his own grief and guilt.

"I'm sorry, Grace," he said, his voice heavy with regret. "I know I haven't been there for all of you like I should be. But that doesn't excuse what you did tonight."

Grace's anger flared once more, her voice trembling with emotion. "It's not just about tonight, Dad. It's about everything. Mom's gone, and you're ... you're not the same anymore. I don't feel like I can depend on you for anything. You work all the time, and it's like we are on our own, unless Aunt Blair is here. I'm sixteen, Dad. I shouldn't be raising a baby! That's *your* job!"

Caleb's heart lurched at her words, the truth of them hitting him like a punch to the gut. "I know, Grace. I'm trying, I really am. But it's hard to think of anything other than your mother's disappearance."

Her expression looked suddenly thunderous. "That's what I'm talking about. Don't you get it? It's not about Mom's disappearance. It's about *her death*. The sooner you accept that, the sooner you can move on and at least give us back one parent. And if you keep running Aunt Blair off, she's going to stop coming and we'll have no one."

With that, she turned and stormed up the stairs, leaving Caleb sitting at the counter, his head in his hands. He felt utterly lost, unsure of how to mend the growing chasm between him and his daughters.

He heard Zoey begin to cry and, slowly, feeling at least a hundred years old, he stood and went to her room. He gathered her up in his arms and began to pace the floor, the weight of his responsibilities pressing down on him like a crushing load.

His daughters needed more.

Hell, they deserved more.

But it was more than he could give right now. Lydia needed him more than anyone else and that hurt him to even think it, because that fact was hurting the girls he loved. Before now, he'd never known that the human heart could carry so much pain and keep beating.

He also couldn't stop the thoughts that maybe his children would be better off if he was gone, too. If he went ahead and joined Lydia, so they could be together, and the girls could have a guardian that wouldn't be such a sad slob. Someone who would raise Zoey with joy and laughter, not drag sadness with them everywhere they went. Maybe Blair moving in wouldn't be such a bad idea after all.

CHAPTER 22

*T*he Greyhound bus rattled along the highway, each bump and jostle adding to Allison's stress as she struggled to pacify her tired and fussy children. They were two hours into the trip and Chelsea was starting to wear down. Her excitement over getting into the big bus had worn off, making her grumpy as she tugged at Allison's arm, insisting to be held, while Toby squirmed in her lap.

"Honey, I can't hold both of you at the same time," Allison said. "Wait until he goes to sleep, and I'll put him in his carrier."

Chelsea whined louder, and Allison could feel the eyes of the man seated next to them as he grew increasingly impatient. She couldn't blame him. He obviously hadn't meant to buy a ticket next to a stressed-out mother and her two needy children. He also didn't know they were running for their lives, or maybe he'd be a bit more sympathetic, but Allison wasn't about to inform him.

Just as her daughter's cries reached a crescendo, the man let out an exasperated sigh and muttered a curse under his breath. Then Allison smelled a whiff of evidence that Toby needed a diaper change.

Lord, what else? Please give me a break here.

She couldn't leave Chelsea in the seat next to the stranger, and she didn't think Chelsea would go with her, either, not in the mood she was in. Most likely the whole bus was about to get a front row seat to an epic meltdown by the cutest two-year-old they'd probably ever seen.

Allison's cheeks flushed with embarrassment, but, before she could apologize again, an elderly woman appeared beside them. She was dressed quite colorfully for a senior citizen, Indian jewelry hanging from her neck and in bracelets around her wrists. The vibrant shawl she wore looked crocheted and included every color of the rainbow. Her hair was gray, but with a streak of black from each temple leading up to the bun that sat high atop her head.

"Would you like to switch seats with me, sir?" the woman asked the man, her voice soft and polite. "I'm right up front and the driver has a wonderful audio book playing."

He nodded eagerly, gathered his belongings, and retreated to the seat up front.

Allison breathed a sigh of relief as the woman settled into the vacated seat, her big bag thudding against the floor.

"Thank you," Allison said, feeling a weight lift off her shoulders.

"No worries." The woman smiled kindly and pulled a baggie of cookies from her bag, offering one to Chelsea. "Here, sweetheart. Would you like a chocolate chip cookie? My neighbor baked them just this morning to send with me today."

Chelsea's eyes widened, and she looked at Allison for her permission, then reached eagerly for the treat.

Allison was relieved to have something to distract her. Chelsea had already tired of the coloring book and crayons and other books that Mabel had sent with her.

"Thank you so much," she said again, her voice filled with gratitude.

"Oh, please," the woman said, waving away Allison's words. "I'm just doing what anyone would do if they had any compassion for others. They can't help it that they are tired and ready to be in a bed. I'm Cora Wallace, by the way."

"I'm Allison," she replied, offering her hand.

Their conversation flowed easily, but, when Cora asked if Allison was getting off in Atlanta, she hesitated for a moment before replying.

"No, I'll be staying on for a while. I'm going to visit my dad."

Cora nodded understandingly. "He must be so excited to see his grandchildren."

Allison bit her lip, feeling guilty for not being entirely truthful. "Actually, it's the first time he'll be meeting them," she admitted, her voice barely above a whisper. "I'm ... I'm leaving a bad situation, and he's helping me out."

Cora's eyes softened with sympathy, and she reached out to pat Allison's hand. "You're doing the right thing, dear," she said, her voice filled with conviction. "You're strong, and you're a good mother. Everything will work out in the end."

Tears pricked at the corners of Allison's eyes as she nodded. She hoped the prediction was true. It was a real turn of events going from not knowing where her father even lived, to her mother telling her she knew, then calling him and setting up an impromptu visit. Her mother claimed that she'd only recently found out and just happened to have his number, and that no one would ever think to look for her in Tennessee.

Wyatt shouldn't, that was for sure. All he knew about her father was that he left when Allison was a toddler.

Allison didn't have the time or the energy to dwell on the revelation that her mom knew where her dad lived and had his number. Getting her kids to safety was more important than starting a battle of words.

Mabel had offered to send her to another shelter in her

network, and that would've been a good alternative, but Allison had to admit that her curiosity was stirred about her father.

Suddenly, Chelsea crawled from her seat onto Cora's lap, causing the woman to chuckle and help her on over.

"Oh, I'm sorry," Allison said. "Chelsea, no. Sit in your own seat, please."

Cora held her hand up. "No, it's okay with me if it's okay with you. It's been a long time since I've had the joy of a child on my lap. This will be a treat for me."

She looked harmless enough and Allison could really use the help, so she nodded.

As Chelsea nestled into Cora's lap, her cries finally subsiding for good, Allison couldn't help but feel a pang of longing for the grandmotherly figure her kids didn't have but so desperately needed.

Toby fussed quietly and Allison watched as Cora draped her shawl over Chelsea, her heart swelling with gratitude for the unexpected kindness. The woman was a Godsend and Allison wished she'd stay with them the entire trip.

"Would you mind watching Chelsea while I use the restroom?" she asked, her voice hesitant. "I'll take Toby with me and change him while I'm in there."

Cora smiled warmly. "Of course, dear. Take your time."

Allison was quick about it, surprised that, even in the tiny space, she was able to juggle Toby while she did her business, wash her hands, then change his diaper and wash her hands again. Returning to her seat, she found Chelsea fast asleep in Cora's arms, her cherubic face peaceful in repose. Gratitude flooded Allison's heart as she thanked Cora yet again, overwhelmed by the unexpected kindness of a stranger.

"You must have grandchildren," Allison said, smiling at the way Chelsea looked totally relaxed in Cora's lap.

"No, I actually don't. I wasn't blessed with children, either, but I've had plenty of nieces and nephews over the years. Their parents have always been glad to let me borrow them here and there. Especially a set of twin grandnieces that I'm especially fond of. Mind you, they're now busy adults and I don't see them much."

That was a shame. Allison wondered if the twins knew how lucky they were to have their Aunt Cora.

"My brother lives in Atlanta and just had hip surgery. He's an old bachelor, and guess what that means? I'm going to go take care of him and his cats while he recovers," Cora added, chuckling. "But I don't mind. His house is very close to a small park and I'm looking forward to taking my knitting there on the sunniest afternoons. If he's not being too ornery for me to leave him alone, that is. He's always given me a bit of trouble when we were growing up."

As the bus rumbled on toward their destination, Cora shared stories of her own life, painting a picture of a woman who had lived some interesting adventures. She seemed to pick up on the fact that Allison didn't want to share her own personal business and didn't seem to mind hearing about hers.

Cora's conversation was making Allison feel normal.

In that moment, she couldn't help but feel a bit of envy for the life that Cora had lived, and she wondered if she would ever have adventures of her own to speak of. Ones that didn't include fear, betrayal, and going week to week just trying to survive.

CHAPTER 23

The bus finally pulled into the station in Chattanooga, Tennessee, and Allison was instantly so nervous, she felt like she could throw up. That would have to wait, because right now she needed to be strong for her kids.

"Chelsea, wake up," she said, prodding her daughter gently with the arm that wasn't holding Toby. "We're here."

The kids were both exhausted, and Allison was, too, but she gathered them and stepped off the bus. She scanned the crowd, unsure of what her father looked like. Her mother only had old photos, and Allison hadn't seen her dad since she was probably three or four.

She didn't even know what to look for. For all she knew, he could be a snaggle-toothed hillbilly by now.

Looking around, she didn't see anyone even close to what she was expecting, but they were fifteen minutes early, so maybe he wasn't there yet.

While they waited on their suitcases to be pulled off the bus, her mind reeled with possibilities that could've kept him from showing up.

He ran out of gas. His car broke down. He went to the wrong station.

He didn't want to see her.

That was the one that was anchored in her mind. The fact that he lived only a few hours from her over the state line kept ringing in her ears. He could've come looking for her any time over the last twenty years. He could've found her on Facebook.

She would ask him about it right to his face.

Then she could watch his eyes and see if he tried to make up a reason, or if he simply admitted that his abandonment of her was just something he did on purpose, with no thought of how he'd made a little girl wonder why everyone else in her classes had a daddy, but she didn't. Why—on Father's Day—it was just another afternoon, when others were celebrating, and why when Chelsea had asked where her grandpas were, Allison had nothing to tell her.

Allison's mother said he had gone back to his first wife, the one who came before he'd met her and had Allison.

The tattered suitcases that Mabel had given her were finally set out and Allison took them one-by-one—holding Toby in his carrier with one arm—to the bench they'd claimed.

"Mommy, I'm hungry," Chelsea whined.

"We'll get something soon." She was down to her last three hundred dollars and had no idea if they might need it for a motel room if her dad didn't show.

Cora, bless her soul, had left numerous snacks with them when she'd disembarked in Atlanta, along with her phone number in case Allison ever needed it. Chelsea had cried, not wanting the old woman to leave her, and the only thing that had stopped her tears was letting her pig out on all the cookies at once. The only thing left was a few granola bars that she knew her daughter would turn her nose up at.

Finally, a man approached them. He was handsome.

"Allison?" he asked tentatively.

She nodded and looked relieved. He had a rugged, rustic charm about him, dressed in faded jeans and a worn cowboy hat. His weathered face broke into a shy smile as he awkwardly kissed Allison on the cheek.

"Hey there, I'm Nate," he said, his voice warm and gentle. He knelt in front of Chelsea, handing her a purple, stuffed teddy bear with a sheepish grin.

"This is for you, Chelsea."

She grabbed it and hugged it to her chest. Purple was her favorite color.

Allison noted that her dad didn't quite match the old photos she had seen of him. He was much older, of course. But there was a kindness in his eyes that made her feel at ease. She also saw now where the cleft in Toby's chin had come from.

"I can get the baby and one suitcase, if you can get the other and hold Chelsea's hand," he said.

Relieved to finally have someone else to hold Toby, Allison handed him in his carrier over to Nate. He grabbed one of the suitcases in his other arm and led them out to the parking lot, where a beat-up pickup truck awaited them.

As they drove out of Chattanooga and into the countryside, Nate pointed out a few landmarks along the way. Martin Hotel. A famous old cannon. The Tennessee River, which was of particular interest to Chelsea.

Nate explained to her how he had taken tubes that looked like big donuts and floated them on the water.

Allison listened intently, glad he was filling the silence as she took in her surroundings and snuck a few glances at him.

Who had he ridden the river with?

She didn't even know if he had other kids.

"And I think there's a space in my house that one little girl is going to love," he said, his words trailing off with a tease.

Chelsea grinned, practically jumping up and down in her seat.

Allison couldn't get over how nice he was. He sure didn't act like the guy her mother had often described in derogatory terms over the years. She'd had every right to do so, though, considering how he'd left them high and dry.

Eventually, they were out in the country and Nate turned down a dirt road, then onto a long driveway. She braced herself, fully expecting that he lived in a squalid trailer park or something similar.

He pulled up in front of a modest log cabin. Two rocking chairs graced the front porch, along with a huge stack of firewood. Toward the back of the yard, she could see a barn and a chicken coop, but chickens ran free. A line of tall pines posed a formidable background for it all, with the tips of mountains peeking over them.

Two huge white dogs lay calmly on the porch, their tails wagging furiously.

"Well, this is it," he said, his words humble but with a tiny sliver of pride. "That's Aspen and Argo. They keep the coyotes away."

Allison made a mental note not to let Chelsea out of her sight.

Nate turned off the truck, then helped her get the kids out, setting Toby and his carrier on the porch before coming back for the suitcases.

"You can go on in. I don't lock it up," he called out.

He was going to have to change that habit once she told him about Wyatt.

Inside, the decor was simple and masculine, the furniture worn leather and the rugs colorful braided pieces scattered about.

"Go up those stairs," Nate said, nudging Chelsea.

"Hold on to the railing," Allison said.

She followed her daughter, to be surprised by a loft packed full of books. She realized she'd already pigeonholed him into a Tennessee country boy who only loved to hunt and drive trucks.

"Mommy!" Chelsea called out. "Look!"

She perched herself inside a reading alcove that was built into the slanted ceiling. A soft blanket and an assortment of pillows made it the perfect place to curl up and read or take a nap.

"This will be my bed," Chelsea said, throwing herself back on a pillow.

"Okay, but that means you have to sleep by yourself," Allison warned.

"I don't care."

Allison laughed. Chelsea wouldn't sleep by herself.

Nate came up the stairs.

"What do you think, Ladybug?" he asked Chelsea, making her blush with pleasure. "I also have a tire swing in the backyard and, after we eat some dinner, I'll take you out there."

Allison felt like she was dreaming. Here was a man who, on the outside, appeared to be the epitome of a father that she had always wanted to have and now he was calling her daughter "Ladybug" and winning her over with a book nook and a swing.

There was also a little bit of anger inside her.

Anger simmering just below the disbelief.

Maybe even boiling. She would have preferred he not look so perfect. It would've made it easier to get over the fact that he'd not bothered to be a part of her life. She couldn't imagine what he would tell her that would justify the fact that she grew up without a father when he was right there and appeared to be a normal person.

It wasn't the time to stir up trouble, though. They had nowhere else to go.

Answers could wait. The safety of her children came before the affairs of her heart.

"This is a nice place, Nate," Allison said. "Thank you again for having us. I promise it won't be for long. I just need a few weeks to get on my feet."

"Hey, there's no timer," he said. "Anyway, why don't you and the kids freshen up and I'll put on some hot dogs and mac and cheese. That was the best bet for options until I figure out what you all like to eat."

"That's perfect. We aren't picky. Thanks."

"Your room is down the stairs; take the hallway, and it's the first door on the right. I've already put your suitcases in there. Towels and soap are stocked in the bathroom if you need them."

With that he went down the stairs and to the kitchen. Allison heard cupboards opening and pots and pans being plunked down.

She couldn't wait to get her traveling clothes off. She hoped to never have to be on a bus long distance again.

"Chelsea, I'm going to go take a bath with Toby. Please come down in a few minutes and find Mommy, okay?"

"Okay," she said, not lifting her head from a small book with a mouse on the front.

Nate must've gone out and bought it the night before.

Or did he have young kids? He wasn't so old that it was impossible. Maybe he'd hooked up with some young floozy and popped out a few kids to be a weekend dad to.

WHEN THE THREE of them were clean and in fresh clothes, Allison led Chelsea out of the bedroom and to the kitchen. Toby was on her shoulder, rooting around in his hunger. Chelsea was biting at the bit to get back out there and see Nate.

Nate was at the stove, stirring a small pot.

"Who's hungry?" he asked, smiling.

"I am," Chelsea said, a little too enthusiastically.

"Y'all have a seat at the table. I'll bring it over."

"I just need a minute to make up a bottle for Toby," Allison said, slinging the diaper bag onto the countertop. "Do you have filtered water?"

Nate set the two pots and a pack of buns on the table, then turned back to her.

"I picked some up. If you'll allow it, I can take him while you eat. I haven't made a bottle in decades, but I can read directions, and I have common sense."

He looked so earnest.

And now that she'd had a bath, Allison was feeling even more exhausted. She wanted to sit down.

"If you're sure?" she asked tentatively.

His answer was in the action of him crossing the room, taking Toby from her, and balancing him easily on one shoulder while he looked into the diaper bag and brought out the can of formula and a bottle.

Allison felt frozen in place.

No one ever helped with her kids.

"Go," he said, nodding toward the dining nook. "Make Chelsea a plate before she turns the table into a trampoline."

When Allison looked, she took off running for the table, pulling Chelsea down just before she had both knees up in her quest to grab a wiener.

"I got it, girl. Sit down." Quickly, she made up a hot dog with a thin line of ketchup just like Chelsea liked. She added a heap of mac and cheese to the paper plate and pushed it closer to her daughter. "Sorry. Terrible twos, they say."

"Nah. Just a kid learning her independence," Nate said. "Juice boxes in the fridge."

He shook the bottle in his hand to mix the water and powder thoroughly. Then he popped it into the middle of a saucepan of water that he already had warming.

Allison went to the fridge and got a juice box, one eye on Nate to see how long he'd heat the milk for, and to make sure he tested it for hot spots. She wasn't going to admit that she usually used the lazy way and heated it in the microwave. She knew better, but sometimes it was just easier.

Back at the table, Chelsea had already eaten a huge bite of her hot dog and had smeared the ketchup across her chin. Allison wiped it with a paper towel that Nate had set out as napkins, and she sneaked a look at him taking the bottle from the pan.

He gave it a gentle shake, then tested it on the inside of his wrist before bringing it and Toby to the table. He sat down with him, and it took him a few seconds and positions, but he finally made Toby comfortable in the crook of his arm and gave him the bottle.

Toby sucked greedily and Allison finally felt like she could make her own plate. She hurried, hoping her dad couldn't hear the deep rumble that had already started in her belly. The few of Cora's cookies left after Chelsea was done were long gone in her digestion.

"Hungry little fellow," Nate said. "Eats with gusto, like his grandpa."

Allison raised her eyebrows. "Is that what you want to be called?"

He realized what he'd said and looked embarrassed.

"I mean—that's up to you. The kids don't know me so if you'd rather they didn't—well ... that's ... I mean ..."

"It's fine, Nate," she said, putting him out of his misery. "I feel it's disrespectful to call grandparents by their first names so Grandpa it is."

He nodded and she could tell he was trying not to smile.

"Want me to make you a plate?" she asked him.

"Nah, that's okay. I'll get Toby all settled first. I'm not too hungry anyway."

Luckily, as Allison ate and Nate stayed busy with Toby, Chelsea filled the gap with nonstop babbling, telling Nate about the big bus, and Miss Cora, and the man sitting in front of them.

"He farted," Chelsea said, then wrinkled her nose. "Phew-wee."

Nate laughed, deep from his belly. "You're something else," he said to Chelsea, still giggling.

She beamed back, mac and cheese showing in her open mouth.

Allison wondered if he'd ever been that enamored with her when she was her daughter's age. Before he'd shut the door and left her forever. She had so many questions. Not only about their past, but, also, his present. *Had he married? Was he with someone now? Kids? Grandkids?*

Things an adult daughter should already know about her father.

"I want swing?" Chelsea asked suddenly.

"You mean, what about the swing, Grandpa?" Allison corrected.

"G—Grandpa, I want swing," she said, stumbling over the word Grandpa.

Allison and Nate laughed.

"I'll take Toby and lay him down, then meet you guys out there," Allison said. Toby's eyes were now shut since his belly was full.

"You finish your food, girls. Or no swing," Nate said, winking at Allison.

And if Allison didn't know any better, she'd think her dad was on a mission to charm her socks off.

CHAPTER 24

*T*aylor stood on the doorstep of a modest suburban home with Caleb beside her, the air heavy with anticipation as they waited for someone to answer their knock. She couldn't shake the feeling of apprehension that coiled in the pit of her stomach, having grown heavier with each mile of the more than four hours it took for them to get to Birmingham, Alabama.

The door swung open, revealing a middle-aged woman with weary eyes and a haunted expression. "Oh my God. Did you find her? Did you find Jill?" she exclaimed, her voice trembling with emotion.

Taylor exchanged a glance with Caleb, a flicker of confusion passing between them.

"I'm sorry, Mrs. Addler. We're not here about your daughter," Taylor said gently, her voice tinged with sympathy. "We're from Hart County, Georgia. We need to speak with you about your ex-husband, Norman."

Gwen's eyes widened in surprise, her gaze darting between them as if trying to decipher their intentions. "My last name is not Addler any longer. It's Kelley, but what about him?" she asked, her voice cautious.

"I was there the night you both came to visit Hart's Ridge and stayed in a local short-term rental on the lake a few years ago. We were called because your husband had tried to choke you," Caleb said.

"I dropped those charges," she said, clutching the door frame.

"Please, can we come in?" Taylor asked. "There's another woman in trouble and you might be the only one who can help her."

Gwen sighed, then stood aside. "Might as well. Another uniform standing around won't hurt anything."

They followed her down the entryway and past a kitchen with several law enforcement members around the table, one on his phone, leaning over the kitchen sink as he stared out the window.

Taylor hoped they could talk to Gwen before anyone interrupted and kicked them out of their way and off their case.

Gwen settled them onto a small couch in an office at the back of the house. It was clear that she was an architect by the draft table and drawings everywhere.

"Thank you for talking to us, Ms. Kelley," Caleb said.

"Please, call me Gwen. How can I help? As you can see, I have my hands full right now trying to find my daughter."

"We understand completely and we'll be quick. We know you decided not to file charges against Norman for domestic abuse that night," Caleb interjected. "We need to know if you have any idea where he might be now."

Gwen's expression darkened, a shadow of fear crossing her features. "I haven't seen him in nearly three years, I guess," she said, her voice barely audible. "That night was the tipping point. I divorced him and took my daughter with me. I don't know where he is now. They've already cleared him as a suspect in Jill's disappearance."

Taylor felt a pang of sympathy for the woman standing before them, a survivor of abuse trying to rebuild her life from the shattered pieces of her past.

"Can you tell us a little about Norman? What kind of man is he?" Taylor asked.

Gwen's eyes flickered with pain as she looked between them, her gaze haunted by memories of the past. "He ... he was charming at first," she began, her voice hesitant. "He was attentive, seemingly generous. But, as time went on, he changed. He became detached, like I was living with a stranger."

Taylor nodded, her heart heavy with the weight of Gwen's words. She had heard stories like this before, tales of love turned sour, of dreams shattered by the harsh reality of abuse.

"He was very shallow," Gwen continued, her voice growing stronger with each word. "He never had anything interesting to say, but he covered that up with jokes and laughter if we were around other people. They never suspected, most of the time. It was like he was wearing a mask, hiding the emptiness inside."

"When did he turn abusive?" Caleb asked.

"A few years into our marriage when I started realizing he wasn't who I thought he was, and I began asking questions," Gwen went on, her voice shaking with emotion. "He doesn't like to be challenged. He used sex as a reward at first, and a punishment later in our marriage if I spoke up or demanded accountability. He made me feel like I was nothing, like I was his property to do with as he pleased. It got to where he forced me to do degrading things that I didn't want to do."

Taylor listened in horror as Gwen recounted the nightmare of her marriage, her words painting a picture of psychological and emotional torment. It was a story she had heard far too many times before, a tale of innocence betrayed, and trust shattered.

Gwen continued. "Then he changed. He was no longer detached, and it was like living in a nightmare. He became domineering, controlling every aspect of my life. Even when he wasn't there, the threat of his return hung over me like a dark cloud, never allowing me to relax or take a moment for myself. I gave up everything. My work. My hobbies and passions. He didn't like it when I pursued my interests, said I was too opinionated and 'aggressive.' So, I stopped. I gave up everything. I even put my education on hold, but I refused to let him take that from me entirely. I finished a master's degree after he was gone, and I'm working on another one now."

"Good for you," Caleb said. "No one should ever stop someone from pursing something for themselves."

"He drove his brother to commit suicide," Gwen added.

"How so?" Caleb asked.

"Talked him into putting his life savings into some venture that had to do with a device that would provide free energy, without needing fuel or an outside energy source."

"I've heard about those scams," Caleb said. "The idea sounds like a dream for those living off grid, but such a contraption doesn't exist."

She nodded. "Exactly. His brother lost everything and couldn't face the humiliation of his failure. Norman didn't invest much. Instead, he let his brother take the loss and never felt a bit of remorse."

"Sounds like an upstanding guy," Taylor mumbled.

"Make no mistake. Norman is dangerous," Gwen said, her voice low and warning. "Don't think for a second that he won't hurt whoever it is you are trying to help. But we haven't had any contact in over a year. I'll admit, he was my first thought when Jill went missing, but the FBI swears he's not a person of interest. And as much as Norman did to me, I can honestly say that he never hurt our daughter. She was off limits when it came to his rages."

"Please think hard, Ms. Kelley. Do you have any idea of places he's gone to before to hang around, or to hide out?" Taylor asked gently. "Somewhere you think he might go?"

Gwen hesitated for a moment; her brow furrowed in thought.

"He might be at his parents' house," she said finally, her voice tinged with uncertainty. "They live out in the countryside, near Springer Mountain in Ellijay. So far up the mountain that they don't have television or internet. I can give you the address. The team went there, too, but he wasn't there when they searched and questioned his parents."

Taylor and Caleb exchanged a glance, a silent agreement passing between them. "The address would be helpful."

Gwen got up and left the room.

When she returned, she handed Taylor a slip of paper. "That's the one I had for them. Keep in mind that they don't like visitors of any kind and probably won't talk to you. If they do, they won't tell you anything because they're protective of Norman. They are a bit weird. Also, I heard through a friend about a year ago that Norman was working at Nebula Law Firm in Marietta, Georgia. Don't know if he's still there. You're welcome to talk to the team here and see what they found out."

"Thank you, Gwen," Taylor said, her voice filled with gratitude. "But we'll check it out ourselves."

"Be careful," Gwen called out as a final warning.

As they made their way back to the car, Taylor felt a rush of anxiety gnaw at her insides. They would check the law firm first before going to visit the parents, especially seeing how Gwen had sounded so serious about how unfriendly the Addlers were. It was all going to have to wait because the day was getting away from them. It had already been more than a year, so Caleb was just going to have to hold on for a few more days.

CHAPTER 25

*L*ydia closed the cover on the book that Dom had given her. She hadn't been able to pace herself and stretch the book out to last longer. It was her third time reading through it, covering every page on tips for survival after every sort of world catastrophe you could think of. She'd never been one to worry about that sort of thing, but there were times now that she hoped for such an event.

Anything to shake up the monotony of her days in the basement.

Luckily for her, she was educated enough to know that the human mind thrived on novelty, so the signs of boredom didn't lead her to spiral into depression like it might someone else. However, it was still a fight for her, even being a professional. But she knew that if she allowed herself to sink to the very bottom of that dark pit that beckoned her, she'd never be able to crawl her way out of it.

She'd be useless to Dom, and he'd quickly end their relationship.

How he'd end it was the question that troubled her. Despite everything she'd been through, she still wanted to live. A person's will to live was usually the last thing to go, and hers was remaining resolute.

At least for now.

But she didn't let herself dwell on how long that would last. A person could only take so much, even when they knew when to spot the trouble spots and turn the other way.

Her long days were tedious, and her brain begged for something to challenge it. For stimulation and a way to test her boundaries. She thought about the bucket list she'd added to over the years. Things like bungee jumping, running a marathon, and visiting the Great Wall of China. She'd dreamed of learning to surf and rock climb and had wanted to one day attend a meditation retreat.

If she ever got out, her bucket list would be different.

She opened the back cover of the book and began to write.

1. **Sell everything, buy a camper, and take family to every state in the USA for sightseeing.**
2. **Volunteer for a needy mission abroad as a family.**
3. **???**

She could only come up with two things and she stared at the words, imagining herself with Caleb and the girls, trekking from one camping site to another on a grand adventure. Cooking marshmallows over the fire. No hot dogs, though.

She'd have to explain that one.

Truly, it didn't matter what they did if she was simply with her family every minute.

Lydia realized that somewhere along the way in her captivity she'd stopped dreaming about building a fat bank account or a dream home. Or traveling to all-inclusive resorts where she could feel fancy for a week out of her life.

She no longer wanted fancy. All she needed was her family around her to be happy.

If she could turn back time, she'd make sure that they spent much more time together as a family, and less time running around to organized sports, to church, or out for date nights. She'd sit on the couch and watch any stupid movie Ella wanted her to, as long as her daughter's head was in her lap and Lydia could run her fingers through her soft hair. She'd let Zoey sleep with them every night, not ever turning away her natural need to be skin-to-skin with her mother. And how fun it would be to teach Grace to drive. She could just imagine the starts and stops, the giggles and the cringing she'd have to hide, but also the celebration after Grace successfully passed her driver's test.

They would've made a mother-daughter day out of it. License, lunch, then nails and toes while they chatted about things that teens liked to talk about.

All the things that would make Grace smile.

Caleb had probably taken her for her test already, and Grace was most likely driving back and forth to school. She wondered what kind of car he'd bought her. She hoped he didn't let Grace drive Ella until she had more experience.

But the meditation retreat she'd once dreamed of—well, that one was covered. She'd taught herself to meditate over the last months, not only during the times that Dom abused her, and she walked herself into her secret room to dance until it was over, but also when she was alone.

It was easy to do now, such a contradiction of her life before when she couldn't find a quiet moment. Now she had plenty of time to sit silent and practice being with herself as she moved from the external world to the internal world where nothing could hurt her, and she felt no grief at the loss of her loved ones and her freedom.

Lydia had learned to take charge of her own mind during those times, keeping a single focus most of the time, and bringing it back to that focus if she strayed.

She roused herself off the mattress and went to the gallon of drinking water. After satisfying her own thirst, she gave Glory a drink. She judged the water level. If her calculations were right, Dom would bring fresh water sometime that evening.

That meant she could use what was left of the clean water to wash her hair. Dom provided her soap and shampoo, since he wanted her to smell fresh, and she leaned over the bucket and poured the rest of her water over her head. She lathered it with shampoo, then rinsed it until most of the shampoo was out. When she'd finished with her hair, she wrapped her one towel around her head, then quickly used the soap and the rest of the water in her bucket to wash her body.

She took the towel off her head and dried herself before putting on a clean dress from the wardrobe cabinet. The material swam around her body, ending at the tops of her ankles, but at least it had been washed and dried. She'd done it herself, of course, with the bar of soap, before draping it from the windowsill for the sun to shine on it.

She was out of food, too, but, along with fresh water, he'd bring something.

Lydia hoped he came soon.

CHAPTER 26

$\mathcal{O}$n Friday, Taylor and Caleb met in the parking lot after their shifts ended, and they headed straight to Marietta. Once they arrived, they approached the law firm where Norman Addler worked; she couldn't help but be impressed by the stateliness of the small building. Tall glass windows adorned the sleek exterior, reflecting the sunlight in dazzling patterns. A polished brass plaque near the entrance proclaimed the firm's prestigious name in bold letters.

Upon entering, they were greeted by a receptionist, a beautiful and young black woman who looked a bit too eager to help, as though she'd been bored and was thrilled someone had walked in.

"We're here to speak with Norman Addler," Caleb announced, flashing his badge. "It's urgent."

Her demeanor instantly changed, a cloud coming over her face. She glanced at the badge, then down at a sheet of paper in front of her. It looked like it held a list of names with checkmarks beside some of them. "I'm sorry, Mr. Addler isn't in at the moment," she said, her voice cool and professional.

"Okay, but we need to speak with someone in authority," Taylor said. "Legal business."

She hesitated for a moment before picking up the phone. She hit a key and then spoke softly, before putting the receiver back down.

"Follow me," she said, leading them down a corridor lined with sleek offices.

They were ushered into a small meeting room, furnished with a mahogany table and leather-padded chairs. A whiteboard adorned one wall, and a phone sat in the middle of the table, silent and unassuming.

Moments later, a senior attorney entered the room, his demeanor one of confidence and authority. "I'm David Nebula," he introduced himself, taking a seat at the head of the table. "What can I do for you?"

"We're interested in speaking with Norman Addler about a case we're working on," Caleb explained.

Nebula arched an eyebrow. "What case?"

"It's confidential," Caleb replied cryptically.

Nebula's expression tightened slightly. "I'm aware of all cases taken at this firm," he stated, his tone bordering on defensive.

"It's not a case Mr. Addler or your firm was hired for," Taylor clarified, watching his reaction closely.

Nebula's confusion was palpable. "I see," he muttered, his gaze shifting uncomfortably. "Well, Mr. Addler is currently taking some time off. I'm afraid I don't know the specifics."

"We need his home address from his files," Caleb pressed, his voice firm. "This is an urgent police matter."

"You really don't know, do you?" he asked.

"Know what?" Taylor said.

"The FBI was already here a few days ago. They went through Addler's office, and even mine. Didn't find a thing."

Taylor had figured that they would've come.

"We're conducting our own investigation into a separate issue," she said.

Nebula hesitated before nodding slowly. "I'll have Freya, the receptionist, bring you his address. Feds got that, too. But I'm late for a deposition and Addler has caused me enough of my billing time," he said, rising from his seat and exiting the room.

While they waited, a woman peeked her head into the room, her eyes scanning the occupants before stepping inside and shutting the door behind her.

She introduced herself as Rachel, a partner at the firm.

"I overheard you asking about Norman Addler," she began, her voice low and cautious. "Is he in trouble?"

"We can't give out any information," Taylor replied carefully. "But if you know something about him that you'd like to share, we'd appreciate it."

Rachel leaned in, her expression grave. "Hmm. What can I say? He thinks he's the boss of me, but we are on the same level. On the rare times I'm forced to work with him, getting him to do his part is like trying to get blood out of a stone," she confided. "David likes him because he brings in the money, but the truth is, Norman only cares about his own agenda and will do anything to further it, even if it means throwing the firm under the bus. He's already made two paralegals and three receptionists quit, but David doesn't seem to realize, or doesn't want to, that Norman is the common denominator of each dramatic episode."

Taylor nodded, absorbing Rachel's words. "Is he married? Or dating someone?" she inquired.

Rachel shook her head. "I don't know any names, but he's usually only interested in one-night stands," she revealed. "And he's always talking about hiking the Appalachian Trail like he's some kind of professional outdoorsman. I bet the first time he comes face-to-face with a bear, he'll shit himself."

Rachel really didn't care for Norman, it seemed.

Caleb jumped in. "What else is he interested in?"

Rachel sighed. "He's obsessed with the idea of the world shutting down and everyone having to fend for themselves," she admitted. "Rumor has it his father was some sort of crazy prepper."

As they processed Rachel's revelations, Taylor and Caleb exchanged a glance, a silent understanding passing between them. They had a clearer picture of Norman Addler now, but they were still far from finding Lydia.

When they heard the click-clacking of heels coming down the hall, Rachel bade them a quick goodbye and slipped out.

The receptionist returned and handed Caleb a slip of paper.

"That's Norman's address," she said.

"I'm sorry, but we didn't get your name," Taylor said, before she could slip back out of the room.

"Freya." She said, smiling nervously.

"Oh, that's right. Mr. Nebula did tell us your name. How long have you worked here, Freya?"

She looked too smart to be doing a receptionist job at the swanky law firm, but Taylor could feel the nerves coming off her in waves. She was hiding something.

"Oh, about five months, I think," Freya said.

Taylor thought the woman had probably been hired through a staffing service. Receptionist positions were like a revolving door when it came to high stress environments.

"I'm just working here while I'm finishing school. When I graduate, they might offer me a paralegal position," she said.

"So, you know Norman, too?" Caleb said. "What can you tell us about him?"

Freya blushed scarlet.

That blush said a lot, and Taylor was picking up every bit of it.

"You went out with him, didn't you?" she asked.

"I—I um—" she stuttered, looking up the hall as though hoping for someone to save her.

Taylor held her hand up. "Listen, you are not in any kind of trouble. Whatever you say will even be off the record, but, please, we are just trying to get a feel for Norman. Did you go out with him?"

"Just once," Freya said. "I know that's bad—and please don't tell David. It's just that, well, he wouldn't leave me alone and I thought that he would fire me if I said no. I really need this job. So, it was just dinner one night."

Caleb stood slowly and beckoned for Freya to come into the meeting room. She did so, but her body language suggested that it was grudgingly.

He shut the door softly, then sat back down. "How did it go? Did he act unusual in any way? Did you go to his home?"

Suddenly Freya burst into tears. Taylor jumped up from her seat and went to her, pulling her into an embrace.

"It's okay, Freya. What did he do?"

Freya told them, through tears as she tried to get herself under control.

"He took me to Pappadeaux, even though I told him I don't eat seafood. Then he insisted that I drink three glasses of red wine. I don't usually drink but he was very persuasive. Afterward, I remember him driving me home and taking my keys from me to unlock the door. He came in with me and that's about all I can tell you, except—" she burst into tears again.

"Except what?" Taylor urged. "It's okay. You can tell us."

She sniffled and then looked up at Taylor, avoiding Caleb, it seemed.

"Except that all I was wearing when I woke up was my socks. I always sleep in pajamas. I could tell I'd had sex because my body was sore, but I could only remember it like it was snapshots in a dream. I was so mortified that I almost didn't come back here. But, like I said, I need this job. The next Monday morning, Norman acted like nothing had ever happened. He has treated me coldly since then. Doesn't even look at me when he comes in the door."

"I'm so sorry that happened to you," Taylor said. "As you may already know, that's called date rape, Freya, and it's not your fault. If you decide to file a report, I'll walk you through it at your local police department."

Freya looked horrified and shook her head emphatically.

"No, I don't. I don't want my family to know and I just want to forget it. It's my fault because I shouldn't have been drinking. And I guess I gave him my keys and asked him to come in. No— I'm not doing that."

"Just so you know, that's a textbook response from someone who has been date raped," Taylor said softly. She pulled her card from her pocket and scribbled her phone number on the back. "If you change your mind, call me. I'll come back up here and help you."

Freya looked relieved that they weren't going to press it. She took the card and backed toward the door.

"I really need to get back up there before David notices I'm gone," she said, then she slipped out, leaving the door ajar.

"Now what?" Caleb said, leaning back in the chair. "We've got his address but if he's there, I doubt he'll let us in. Without a search warrant, we're stuck."

"And we have nothing that will convince a judge to give us a search warrant," Taylor added, feeling defeated. "I guess it's time to visit Mommy and Daddy Addler."

They heard footsteps again, this time heavy. As they listened, Nebula walked by, not even looking their way in his hurry to get to the lobby area.

"I'm taking a long lunch, Freya. Hold my calls," he said. Then they heard the front door swing open and shut.

Taylor stood. "On second thought, we could check out his home first and talk to some neighbors. Never know, maybe he's there and will be cordial."

"I doubt that."

Taylor and Caleb turned to the door.

Rachel was back and she was shaking her head.

"Don't bet on it. Cordial is saved for when Norman wants to romance the jury. For the rest of us, the most we expect is a robotic response tinged with disdain. But if you want, I can show you his office."

CHAPTER 27

*A*llison jolted awake, her heart pounding in her chest as she heard the voices in the kitchen. For a moment, panic seized her, her mind racing to the worst-case scenario.

Wyatt.

He must have followed her here.

Terror ran through her, and she threw off the covers and dashed down the hall, her bare feet slapping against the wood floor, breaths coming in short, frantic bursts.

As she burst into the kitchen, relief washed over her in waves, but confusion quickly replaced it. Instead of Wyatt, she found two young women, a man, and two small children seated at the table with Chelsea, who was happily coloring away as though she wasn't surrounded by strangers.

One of the women held Toby in her arms.

Nate stood awkwardly by the stove, looking flustered.

"I came in to wake you for breakfast," he said. "But you were sleeping so well, and the kids wanted up, so we thought we'd let you sleep in. You needed to catch up."

"I changed Toby, so he's all fresh," the woman holding him

said. "But we didn't want to rustle in your room for clean clothes."

Allison's mind raced as she tried to make sense of the scene before her. Toby and Chelsea were still in their sleeping clothes, but Chelsea's hair was neatly combed back into a ponytail. Someone other than her had done her daughter's hair.

Who were these people, and why were they here?

Why hadn't her father mentioned anything about visitors coming?

"I—um—" she crossed her arms over her T-shirt, feeling suddenly vulnerable in her mussed hair and mismatched pajamas in front of the two women who were neatly dressed much prettier than her. "I should go get dressed."

She turned to go.

"Wait, Allison," Nate said. "I'm sorry to spring this on you. I didn't know they were coming," he stammered, his eyes darting between Allison and the newcomers. "They just—"

Before he could finish, the young woman at the table jumped up and rushed over to Allison, enveloping her in a warm hug. "I'm sorry, we should have introduced ourselves immediately. I'm Nova, and this is my husband, Beau." She gestured to the man at the table, who smiled warmly at Allison.

The other young woman looked several years older than Nova. She shyly approached. "I'm Lyla,"

So, this must be her dad's girlfriend.

Lyla.

Allison's heart skipped a beat. She took Toby from Lyla's arms, feeling a surge of resentment toward the woman. She tried to push it down. She didn't know why she would feel that way, but she didn't want her holding Toby.

"Mommy!" Chelsea called out, turning around with a huge smile. "I color you a pretty picture."

"*I'm* coloring you a pretty picture," Allison corrected, barely loud enough for even herself to hear.

Everyone was staring at her.

The two children at the table were dressed in neat clothes, shiny white sneakers on their feet as they pored over their pages. Chelsea's socks didn't match and were the last clean pair she had. Her shoes were in even worse shape.

"I'll be back in a minute or two," she said, then retreated to her room, Toby still cradled in her arms. She paced back and forth, talking to him as she tried to make sense of the whirlwind of emotions swirling inside her.

Toby had a fistful of her hair, and he stared up into her eyes, the corner of his mouth turned up. A wave of love and protection fell over her. She was still not over her irrational first fear that Wyatt had come and grabbed him and Chelsea.

Now that she knew he hadn't found them, something else was bugging her. Nate had all kinds of people surrounding him. He didn't need Allison and her kids.

A soft knock on the door broke her reverie, and she opened it to find Lyla standing there, looking uncertain.

"Can I come in?" she asked softly.

Allison hesitated for a moment before nodding, allowing her to enter.

Lyla perched on the edge of the bed, her eyes searching Allison's face. "Is there anything you want to ask me?" she ventured.

Allison couldn't hold back the question that had been burning in her mind since she first laid eyes on Lyla. "Isn't Nate too old to have kids that young?" she blurted out.

Lyla looked confused only for a second before her laughter filled the room, and Allison felt a flush of embarrassment creeping up her neck. "Oh, gosh," she chuckled. "That's funny. No, those kids aren't Nate's. They belong to Nova and Beau. Nate is our dad. Their grandpa."

Allison tried not to show her shock.

"You've been here for nearly a week, so I would've thought he would've told you about us," Lyla said, her voice tinged with sadness. "I'm sorry that we just burst in today, but he wouldn't answer his phone and we just couldn't wait any longer. We wanted to meet you and the kids."

Allison's mind whirled with questions, but one thought stood out above the rest: her father *had* raised another family, just as she'd suspected. But they were older than her, so he'd raised them first. Or—did that mean she was a love child? Had Nate and her mother had an affair, and he didn't want to leave his family for her?

That made the most sense. She shook her head, trying to process the revelation.

"It must be nice having a father," she said, unable to keep the words inside any longer.

Lyla reached out and placed a gentle hand on Allison's arm. "I know this is a lot to take in, but, please, before you make any rash decisions or judgments, give him time. There's a lot you don't know."

"There's a lot you don't know either," Allison said. "And a lot Nate doesn't know. Like the times I wished I had someone to take to the father-daughter dance at school, other than one of my mom's random boyfriends. Or the times I wish I would've had a dad to scare my boyfriend when he cheated on me with my best friend, and didn't show up for his own child's birth, and stopped seeing her when she was just a baby. I guess he thought he was leaving me to a loving mother, but what I had was someone who took the opportunity to kick me to the curb the first big mistake I made."

Lyla's eyes were swimming with tears when Allison stopped her speech.

"You know what? I'm sorry," Allison added. "It's not your fault. I know at least that much. This has nothing to do with you or your sister. I shouldn't have said anything. He did show up for me this one time, so I guess I can't complain, can I?"

"Maybe," Lyla said, standing and coming to Allison. She put

her hand on her wrist. "But I want you to know that I am so sorry that you didn't have him like we did. And you can talk to me about anything. I understand that you don't know me. Or Nova. But we want to change that if you'll let us."

Allison didn't know what to say to that. She was afraid to let her guard down. Scared to death to believe that anyone related to her would have her best interests at heart. But under the fear were other emotions. Relief that her dad wasn't seeing someone young enough to be his daughter.

And hope.

Hope that maybe life had finally thrown her a bone, and, when all this was over and settled down, she really would have a family that would always have her back.

CHAPTER 28

*T*he drive toward Ellijay started out in silence, the tension thick in the air between them. The sheriff still wasn't sold on them spending any company hours investigating Lydia's case, and Caleb was frustrated about what he felt was nonchalance from those who a year ago had promised to help him through this ordeal.

The only one who had kept that oath was Taylor, and he was thankful for her.

He was driving this segment, and she was currently looking at her phone, navigating the directions to the Addler's property.

"Have you been to Ellijay before?" she asked.

He nodded. "A few times. Lydia dragged me to their Apple Blossom Festival last year. She loved to see all the different art booths while I sampled the food."

"Ellis and Cate took a North Georgia wine-tasting tour a few months ago and had a stop in Ellijay," Taylor said. "I've been up there a few times, just to bump around downtown in the second-hand shops with Jo."

It was a beautiful drive, the countryside lush and green. As a matter of fact, the name Ellijay was thought to mean *place of green things* in the Cherokee Indian language, the people who had inhabited the Indian village when white settlers came to the remote mountain community—before it expanded into a town and the Indians were unfairly removed to Oklahoma.

The silence felt so awkward that soon Taylor began to talk, going back over what they knew so far, which could be a huge break in the case, or could be nothing.

"There's no way he's living in that condo full-time," Caleb said.

Taylor had to agree. Though they hadn't entered the premises, the condo was luckily on the ground level, and a corner of the building. Norman obviously wasn't hiding anything because his blinds were wide open and the floor to ceiling windows gave them a generous look inside, showing not only the open concept main living area, but also the primary bedroom. Everything they saw was spotless. Not a single item out of place, or a crumb on the counter.

Either he or an expensive interior designer had decided to go with a palate of whites and creams, and, to Taylor, it gave it too much of a sterile look. She would have to have some colorful quilts or pillows thrown around to break up the perfectness of too many shades of white. Maybe a few old-fashioned braided rugs scattered about on the floors.

"Crazy, too," Caleb added, "because that place is costing him a pretty penny just to sit there and look pristine."

The condo was in the exclusive Park Ridge community where the cost of a one-bedroom apartment was comparable to what someone would pay for a monthly mortgage on a huge, middle-class house. The condos had their own small garages but in the overflow area of parking, it was full of high-end cars, with Mercedes, BMWs, and even a Range Rover or two.

They'd talked to one neighbor who said she hadn't seen Norman in a month or more, and, before that, he was only there sporadically.

"He never waves back at me," she'd said, a frown making her wrinkles deeper around her mouth as her mood turned sour. "I even took him a package that was delivered to my door instead of his, and he could barely squeeze out a proper thank you. I'm not fond of people like that, especially here in the south where we've learned the proper manners and etiquette of how to act. He gives the rest of us a bad name."

She obviously had a bone to pick with Norman, but she had plenty to say to them, too.

According to her, Norman was a loner. He used the pool and gym in their amenities center, but always with an expression that blocked any efforts of niceties toward him from others.

"For being such a handsome man," she'd said, "he likes to wear a scowl and he never brings home any lady friends. He could meet a few single ladies around here, if he'd deign to join us in playing tennis or pickle ball."

When they'd left the neighbor, Taylor saw her take off toward the community clubhouse, probably to spread the news that Norman Addler had the police looking for him.

"Want to stop here?" Caleb asked, slowing down at the entrance to a small mom and pop restaurant that advertised hot dogs and wings.

"That works if *you're* hungry."

He pulled in and parked. Inside, they both ordered a cheeseburger and fries, but neither of them ate much. They were too eager to get to the Addler's house.

An hour and a half later, they pulled up to a secluded farmhouse nestled at the top of one of Ellijay's mountains. She was reminded of the kidnapping and brutal murder of a thirty-seven-year-old woman committed in the same county a while back.

Nine members of a drug trafficking group had booked a cabin online with a stolen identity, then booked an uber to take them there. The driver was a young woman, and they'd decided to keep her, then tortured her before they killed her, all with the beautiful backdrop of the mountains and the sounds of nature all around them.

Taylor wondered if the cabin that the woman lost her life in was located close by.

"We need to be very careful, Caleb."

"10-4."

Dread settled like a lead weight in the pit of Taylor's stomach.

As they approached the secluded farmhouse nestled among the rolling hills of the countryside, Taylor's apprehension only grew. She couldn't shake the feeling that they were walking into the lion's den, and her gut rarely led her astray.

Caleb parked the car, and they both stepped out, Taylor taking a deep breath to steel herself for whatever lay ahead. They made their way to the front door, Taylor's heart pounding in her chest with each step. When they reached the door, it swung open suddenly, revealing an elderly man with a shotgun in hand.

"Whoa there," Taylor said, her hand going to rest on the firearm on her hip.

"Who are you, and what do you want?" the man barked, his eyes narrowing suspiciously at Taylor and Caleb.

"Sir, please do not aim that weapon at us. We're from Hart County, Georgia," Taylor began, her voice steady despite the tension in the air. "We're looking for your son, Norman. We need to speak with him."

The man's expression darkened, and he tightened his grip on the shotgun, never changing its aim. "I don't know what business you have with him, but you're not welcome here," he growled, his voice laced with hostility. You people have done been here. Leave us alone."

Taylor exchanged a glance with Caleb, silently urging him to keep calm. "We just need to ask him a few questions," Caleb said, his tone placating. "It's important."

The man's lips twisted into a sneer. "Norman works at a fancy law firm somewhere. I suppose he's there," he said dismissively.

KAY BRATT

"We checked. He didn't show up for work," Taylor interjected, her voice firm.

The man's demeanor shifted slightly, a hint of uncertainty flickering in his eyes. "Maybe he's on vacation or something. I don't keep up with his whereabouts," he muttered defensively.

Taylor pressed on. "Does Norman own any other properties that you're aware of? Maybe a cabin or a rental?"

The man shook his head adamantly. "No. Now get off my land before I have to use this here gun. I have signs up saying no trespassing, you know. I can stand my ground and shoot you both."

"Let's go, Caleb," Taylor whispered. "He's off his rocker."

They turned to leave. As they walked back to their car, they took the slow route, scanning the area for any signs of Lydia or Norman. There was no one else about, so they got in and Taylor turned the car around and got back on the main road.

They'd only gone half a mile when—suddenly—a figure stepped out from the woods, causing Taylor to slam on the brakes.

It was an old woman. "Please, don't tell my husband you saw me," she said urgently as she approached the car. "What do you want my son for?"

So, this was Mrs. Addler.

Taylor hesitated, torn between the need for secrecy and the urgency of the situation. "We can't tell you all the details, but a woman's life could be in danger," she said carefully.

Mrs. Addler sighed, shaking her head in resignation. "I always knew he would do something one day that he couldn't undo," she murmured. "He was here, a few days ago. I saw him carry his hiking pack into the barn. I assume he was here to stock up on a few things."

"Was there anyone with him?" Caleb asked.

She shook her head.

"Did he say where he was going?"

"I didn't talk to him. I just saw him through the window when

168

he came up on the porch to talk to his father, then I watched him go to the barn."

"Don't you usually talk to your son when he comes for a visit?" Taylor asked.

A flash of sadness went over the woman's eyes before she answered.

"Not since he grew up," she said. "He doesn't have any love for me, and I've stopped thinking of him as the boy I raised. He's a bad one. I hate to say it, but I don't know *this* Norman."

"Where does he usually like to hike, Mrs. Addler?" Taylor asked, her tone comforting. "Please, Mrs. Addler. It's life or death."

The old woman sighed, and it looked like all the energy she carried was suddenly sucked out of her. "Well, he says I'm dead to him, so I guess I shouldn't feel bad about this. He hikes all over Georgia and South Carolina, but, if I was a betting woman, I'd wager he's headed to some property on Double Knob Mountain. I've never been there, myself. But it was purchased under my other son's name, Kenneth."

"I'm sorry for your loss, Mrs. Addler."

She nodded sadly. "Kenneth Gene Addler. He was the only chance I had at someone to help take care of us when the day comes that we must leave this mountain. Kenny was a good son, but Norman ruined that, too."

With that, Mrs. Addler walked away from the car, leaving Taylor and Caleb staring at the place between the trees that she so nimbly disappeared through, like an ancient wood nymph, there one minute and gone the next.

CHAPTER 29

*A*llison had lived in the south all her life and, surprisingly, had never seen a rodeo, so she could barely contain her excitement when she buckled Toby's carrier into Nate's truck, then got Chelsea settled into the back before taking the front passenger seat.

"Are we there yet?" Chelsea said before they could even get down the long driveway. She was thrilled, too, though all she wanted to talk about was seeing a clown.

"Not yet, Ladybug," Nate said, chuckling.

He had surprised Chelsea with a new outfit of jeans, a red-checkered blouse, and the cutest boots that Allison had ever seen. Chelsea had been stomping around the house in them exclaiming she was a cowgirl for the last two days since he'd brought them home.

"Yee haw," she sang out in every room.

It was a really nice thing for Nate to do. When Allison told him he shouldn't have, he blushed and waved her off, saying it was a tradition for him to buy the grandkids their first boots. He'd offered to take her shopping, too, but Allison declined.

She already owed him so much for taking them in

temporarily. Things were going well, but, so far, Wyatt was still at large, hiding out somewhere like the coward he was.

"I can't wait to get my hands on a corn dog and some deep-fried Oreos," Nate whispered to Allison, winking at her before putting his gaze back on the road.

"Sounds good." Allison loved corn dogs, but the Oreos would be a new treat.

Lyla, plus Nova and her family, were meeting them at the arena. This time when Allison was faced with her sisters, she'd be prepared.

Cleaned up nice and composed, instead of coming off as a nutcase.

After the last fiasco, they'd left quietly while she hid in the bedroom, feeling like an idiot, and Nate had made them swear not to just pop in again.

When Allison had finally emerged from the bedroom, Nate filled her in about Nova and Lyla, telling her at least the basic details of who they were.

"Both the girls did barrel racing when they were in school," Nate said, laughing. "Once they got into boys, they lost interest."

"Girls tend to do that," Allison said. She herself thought she was going to be a real photographer when she was in high school and had even entered some small contests and won prizes. When she got pregnant with Chelsea, that all changed.

Chris Stapleton came on the radio and Nate turned it up.

"Love this song," he said, singing along to the words of *Tennessee Whiskey*.

Allison smiled. That was another thing she had in common with him. Over the last few weeks, she'd found other small quirks that she'd obviously inherited.

At heart, Nate was young. No one would guess that he had three adult children and now four grandchildren. Allison was getting to know this new family, and wishing she'd found them sooner.

Lyla was a hairstylist and had her own spa and salon in downtown Chattanooga. She was single for the moment, after breaking off a long-term engagement. She didn't say it, but Allison got the feeling that, like her, Lyla was unlucky in love.

Nova and Beau were married going on seven years. Their kids, Tommy and Isla, were six and three. He said that Nova fancied herself "a creative," and, aside from staying home to take care of the family, she dabbled in painting, ceramics, and all sorts of other art mediums. Her husband, Beau, worked with Nate as a lineman for one of Georgia's biggest power companies.

It fit. Both Nate and Beau were alpha males, macho in every move they made. They would both look liked caged lions being forced to sit behind a desk all day.

It was strange; until their conversation, Allison hadn't even known what Nate did for a living and really hadn't wondered. Now she couldn't even ride down the highway without looking at the power lines and imagining him climbing a tall pole during a terrible storm.

One evening Nate and Beau were sitting around after dinner, talking about a storm that had hit a few years back, and how all the bucket trucks were in use, so they were on their own when it came to climbing, relying on their hooks and their trust for each other as lookouts.

It sounded like a job that was mentally and physically challenging. Those that did it put their own lives in danger to aid others, and that made her feel something.

Pride? Awe?

She thought over the personality traits she and Nate had in common. They were both more on the introverted side and conversation didn't flow easily between the two of them, unless one of the girls were there to keep it going. They still hadn't gone deep in on any talks about the past, and the more Allison got to know him, the more questions she had.

So far, a girlfriend or significant other hadn't shown up, and

Allison was too embarrassed to ask him about it. She was sure he had someone in his life. He was a good-looking man, had a great job, and a nice home. She couldn't imagine that women weren't chasing after as good a prospect as he seemed to be.

Nate was respectful of her mother, too. He'd not said a bad word about her when her name came up, showing he was much more a gentleman than her mom was a lady, because she loved to use his name as a target for insults and accusations.

Allison truly couldn't imagine them ever being a couple.

Her mom had called her a few times over the last few days. She feigned concern and insisted she needed to know where her grandchildren were and that they were okay. It was too little, too late coming, and Allison knew what she was really after were details about Nate and his life.

Allison only gave her the bare minimum and kept her wanting more. Her mom's latest boyfriend in a revolving door of dozens over the years was on the outs with her again, and Allison had to listen to her mother's ranting about everything he'd done wrong.

In a week he'd be back, and she'd call him her soul mate again.

"We're here," Nate said, pulling into a parking lot—then a space—before cutting the motor. He turned in his seat. "You ready for this?"

Chelsea's head bobbed up and down in excitement.

They climbed out and Nate carried Toby.

Allison took Chelsea's hand. "Do not run away from me, promise?"

"Promise, Mommy."

Allison was nervous bringing a toddler to such a public location packed with people. Her daughter could get lost easily in the sea of heads. Once they were through the ticket booth, she lifted her up and carried her on her hip, following Nate with Toby to their seats in the stands.

She had never seen so many cowboy hats and boots in one place, and everywhere she looked there was something going on.

Nova and her crew were already there and greeted them enthusi-astically. Nova made room between her and the kids and waved Allison to sit by her.

Chelsea squeezed between Tommy and Isla, happy to see them. Isla immediately tore her off a big chunk of blue cotton candy and Allison was thankful she'd remembered to put a new pack of wipes in Toby's diaper bag.

In the arena, things were already starting, and the kids were watching and wide-eyed, watching sheep being let out of the shoots with a kid attached, holding on for dear life.

"William Smith, six years old from Pulaski, is our new leader on the board with six seconds," the announcer called out, and Nova's kids cheered.

It was comical, and cute, too. Listening to Chelsea laugh was everything, after all they'd been through lately.

"I'll take Toby," Allison said, leaning forward so that Nate could see her down the row where he sat next to Beau, Toby cradled happily in his arms.

"Nah, he's fine for now. Relax."

Allison didn't know what to do with her hands without having Toby or Chelsea on her lap. She realized that the kids gave her an armor, protection against feeling awkward around others. Without them as her shield, she felt too vulnerable.

"Oh, I almost forgot," Nova said. "I brought you something."

She dug into her huge bag and pulled out a charcoal gray thingie and handed it over.

"What is this?" Allison asked.

"A chest carrier so you don't have to carry that heavy baby seat when you want to bring Toby inside somewhere."

"Thank you," Allison said. She'd always wanted one of the carriers, but they were pricey. She'd been watching the local Goodwill, hoping one would show up.

"Oh, nice," Nate said. "Hand it down here."

Allison passed it down and watched as Nate handed Toby to

Beau, then put the carrier on, adjusted the straps, then easily slipped Toby into it, facing forward, which immediately pleased him so much that a smile broke out across his face, and he pumped his chubby fists.

"You like that, don't you, little buddy. Now you can watch, too. Might find you're a little cowboy under those rolls of fat," Nate said, his voice carrying down to where Allison sat, watching them. It nearly made her eyes tear up, with thoughts of how that should be Wyatt holding his son, enjoying time with him.

"You okay?" Nova asked her.

Allison wiped at her eyes. "Yeah, got some dust in my eye. I'm going to go down to the bathroom. Can you watch Chelsea?"

Nova nodded and Allison stood and made her way to the end of the row.

"Where're you going, kid?" Nate asked as he slid his long legs sideways to let her pass. "They're about to start the team roping. You don't want to miss that."

"Bathroom." She didn't look him in the eye.

"Oh, well, here," he said, pulling a fifty-dollar bill from his pocket. "Stop by the snack bar on your way back up. Get you and Chelsea whatever you want, just bring me a beer and a corn dog. I'll wait until later for the cookies."

Allison took it, only because she didn't want to stand there and argue with him, and she stepped out of their row and carefully made her way down to the ground. Once there, she made her way through the crowd, following the signs pointing her way to the bathrooms.

She saw Lyla coming at her, but Lyla didn't see her, so Allison quickly darted into the restroom. She needed some time to herself before putting on a happy smile and joining all of them again.

In the bathroom stall, she pulled out her phone and checked her messages. There were a few texts from her mother.

Ran into your manager at Walmart. Call me.

He asked that you turn in your smock and ID card.

Now tears really sprang to her eyes. They'd decided not to save her job after all. While she didn't want Wyatt to go to jail, at least that would've enabled her to go back to Hart's Ridge, find a new place to live, and return to her job.

She was back to being a single mom with no job and nowhere to live. Wyatt would be thrilled because that meant, if she wanted to go back, she'd have to depend on him until she could get her feet under herself again.

A memory of what her face looked like the last time filled her head.

There had to be some way for her to make it without him. Tonight, when she was back at Nate's, she'd call her mom. Beg her to let them come stay, and then call her manager and ask for her job back. Then she wouldn't be starting from scratch.

With that decided, she exited the stall, washed her hands, and left the restroom.

She'd just found the snack bar and gotten in line behind a trio of young girls when she turned around to see what the crowd was cheering for in the arena. She couldn't see well enough over the heads, but, when she turned back around, she saw the back of the head of a guy that was just in front of the three girls.

It was familiar.

She followed the head all the way down to the boots, and every piece of the body was very recognizable. The way he stood, one leg bent, leaning on the other, sent alarm bells ringing in her ears.

No way. He cannot be here. It's impossible.

Just as she was about to talk herself out of it being him, he turned just enough that she saw a dark mole behind his right earlobe.

That was enough.

She nearly dropped to her knees, but she stayed bent below the shoulders of those around her while she backed out of line, then almost ran to the area Nate and the others waited. She flew up the steps and stopped in front of him.

"We have to go," she said. "Wyatt's here."

CHAPTER 30

*A*llison took a deep breath and sent a kick right toward Nate's hip, and he caught her leg mid-air and could've sent her crashing to the ground, but instead held it for a second before dropping it.

"See what can happen there?" he said. "Remember, you have four areas I want you to concentrate on. Eyes, nose, throat, or groin."

She really didn't want to kick her dad in the balls. Something didn't feel right about that, but she backed up and aimed again.

He bent forward and stepped back at the second before contact and saved his family jewels. "Okay, let's try some hammer punches. Here, catch."

He threw his truck keys to her, and she grabbed them in her hand, letting one key protrude between her fingers like a weapon.

She punched at the air in front of his face, over and over.

Her pulse raced and she fought to control her breathing, so she didn't sound like a dog in heat. Nova and Lyla were both lean and trim, their stomachs flat and butts toned. Somehow, they made time in their day for the gym. And they could afford it.

Allison wasn't overweight by any means, but she also wasn't in shape, and she was still carrying her belly weight from Toby.

Considering he was only nearly three-months old, that didn't seem so bad, but she still tried to keep her ragged breaths to herself as she moved.

The rest of the family was inside with the kids, after Allison had begged them not to give her an audience during her first self-defense lesson. Nova tried to tell her that she was just the next one in his line of daughters that he relished teaching his moves to, and not to feel weird about it.

Three days had passed since the rodeo and Allison was still livid at her mother. It didn't take long to figure out how Wyatt knew she was in Chattanooga.

"But he brought over more than a hundred dollars in groceries, Allison," she'd whined. "Even some diapers and formula for Toby. Honey, he's really sorry and just wants to see you and the kids before he goes to jail."

Her mother had no clue the kind of trouble she'd caused, not only to Allison but to Nate and his family. Allison was so furious with her. She hadn't answered any of the texts or calls she'd made since then.

It was humiliating at the rodeo when she'd told Nate that Wyatt was there. He hadn't questioned her or doubted her instincts one bit. Only passed Toby to her, along with his keys and told them to go to the truck, but first to show him a photo of Wyatt.

Allison didn't do it. She was too afraid and just wanted Nate to take them home. Much to her embarrassment, he'd told the rest of the family what was going on and they all decided to leave. Chelsea had thrown one of her atomic tantrums and Nate had ended up having to carry her kicking and screaming, all the way to the truck.

Surely Wyatt heard her screams and had watched them go. Maybe even followed them.

Nate had taught her how to use her elbows as lethal weapons, not only to punch with them if she was face-to-face with an attacker, but also how to get out of a hold if someone grabbed her from behind.

What he hadn't considered, and she didn't remind him, was that most likely if anyone came up on her, she'd be carrying Toby. Then what could she do?

She tried not to think about that scenario.

"Okay, that's enough," he said, then went to the picnic table and sat down "You've worn me out."

She doubted that but was grateful for the cease anyway. "Thanks. I really appreciate the lessons. I hope I don't have to use them."

"Me, too, kiddo. I wish they could find that slimy sucker. It's not fair for you to have to be put in this situation. Those kids need a stable life, not to be uprooted every week. Come here and sit with me for a minute."

Allison sat down opposite Nate.

"What do you think your next steps are?" he asked.

"I'm not sure. I talked to Taylor this morning and she said your local department is on the lookout for Wyatt, but she wants me to stay put until they find him."

She searched his eyes, trying to find a clue what he was thinking. Was he tired of them being there? Maybe he wanted his house back to himself? The girls had come over quite a bit in the last days, but there hadn't been any opportunities for deep talks. Even if there were, Allison didn't think that they would tell her anything about her dad that he wouldn't want them to share.

"In the meantime, what do you think about carrying a weapon?" he asked.

"Like pepper spray?"

He laughed. "No, like a gun. I could help you get licensed to carry."

She paused.

"I'm afraid of guns. I also don't want to have one too accessible to my kids. So, I'd rather not, to be honest," she said.

He nodded. "I respect that. Not everyone feels comfortable with weapons. And in that case, we will get you some pepper spray so that you at least have something. You also need to be careful not to put yourself in dangerous situations where you can't flag down someone for help."

"Yeah, I know. Taylor had a long talk with me this morning about that. But it's not like I have anywhere to go, or any way to go."

"You're welcome to use the car in the garage while you're here," Nate said. "I keep it as a backup to my truck. Never know when an extra vehicle will come in handy."

Allison wouldn't know about having even one dependable car. She only ever had one vehicle at a time, limping along until it died and then she had to scrape up the money to get another clunker.

While you're here, he'd said.

She was saved from analyzing those words too much by Lyla and Nova coming around the side of the house into view.

"Allison," Nova called out. "Go get ready. We're taking you for Sunday brunch. Just the three of us."

Nate smiled broadly, but Allison felt a moment of panic. She didn't know them well enough to enjoy a girls' outing. And she couldn't leave the kids.

"Um ... thank you, but—"

"No buts," Lyla said. "It's already arranged. Dad knows about it, but he wanted to get some lessons in before we left. Go get ready. Wear something cute."

"I can't leave Toby," Allison said.

"Yes, you can. I promise, I've got him," Nate said. "He's due to eat again in two hours and, when he wakes from his nap, I'll change his diaper. Then Beau and I are going to take all the kids on a nature walk. I'll carry Toby on my chest in the carrier. He'll love it." He looked proud of himself.

"See? All handled," Lyla said.

Allison let out a long breath she was holding. She didn't have anything cute to wear, and she really didn't want to leave her kids, but it appeared that she wasn't going to have a choice.

"Okay, give me a few minutes to change," she said, smiling.

＊

TWO HOURS LATER, a server set a huge plate of food down in front of Allison, and her mouth dropped. She'd ordered a Lobster Reuben and steak fries, and it was enough to feed three people.

"I can't possibly eat all this."

Lyla and Nova laughed.

"Dad will eat your leftovers," Nova said. "Beau will eat mine."

They were at Scottie's, a restaurant that overlooked the river downtown. They were at an outside table on the patio, the weather was beautiful, and Allison felt like a fish out of water.

Her sisters were finally calm after a server told them they'd seen the news, and the Facebook-Instagram outage was supposedly just a glitch and being worked on. It had already been out for more than an hour, not that Allison cared.

She wasn't a big fan of social media.

A carafe of mimosa was partially empty in the middle of the table. Allison only sipped at hers, not wanting to arrive back to the house feeling tipsy.

"This is Beau's favorite place for date night," Nova said. "We come every other Thursday night, and he pigs out on the oysters with crawfish sauce."

They dug into their food. Allison was feeling overwhelmed. Not only with spending time with sisters she didn't even know she had less than a week ago, but with how much they'd spoiled her already that day.

"Mmm ... this is great," she said around her mouthful of Reuben. It was her first time trying any kind of lobster.

Lyla owned the Blowology Dry Bar and Spa and had opened the doors on a Sunday just for her. While Allison was getting the ultimate hair treatment from Lyla, Nova was out shopping and returned with a bag from some boutique with a springy outfit in Allison's size.

Allison had tried to resist both the hair day and the clothes, but they'd both insisted that they'd missed out on too many years of being able to spoil a little sister and needed something to keep their minds off checking their phones.

She had to admit, her hair looked better than it ever had. Lyla had shown her how to add so much more volume into it with just a blow dryer and a brush. She'd snipped off the dead ends, too, even though usually the shop didn't do haircuts.

Now Allison was tired. She'd had fun and felt very grateful, but was honestly ready to get back to her kids. She hadn't left them with anyone for this long in a while and it felt unnatural to be without them.

She checked her phone again, looking for a text from Nate, hoping he needed her to come back, stat. Surely Chelsea was crying for her by now?

But there was no such text. Allison yawned, hoping the girls would get the hint. However, listening to Nova talk about date night with her husband was interesting. He worked long hours, and they had two children, but somehow they made it work to make time for them as a couple.

She and Wyatt hadn't done that at all, which might've contributed to the failure of their relationship. It wasn't even just about the time, but people like her didn't have the money for "date night" when they were just scrambling to make ends meet. Or the funds for a babysitter, and the lack of any family members around to do it for free.

Anything they did together included the kids and was usually something free.

Walking through the mall.

Going to a public park.

Swimming in the lake.

It wasn't sitting in a fancy restaurant and drinking cocktails, but they'd made some good memories. One time Wyatt had brought an old jon boat home. He rigged an umbrella over it for Chelsea—it was before Toby was born—and they'd floated around on the lake.

When they got tired, they ate bologna sandwiches that were made that morning and Little Debbie snacks that were packed into a cooler in the back of the van.

Chelsea had loved that outing. She had nothing to compare it to, so, to her, it was a fantastic adventure. One day she'd see a real adventure park like Disney World and realize she'd been cheated in her childhood.

The thought made Allison sad.

Nova's children had probably been to Dollywood, Disney World, and all the others out there that Allison didn't even know the names of. For all she knew, they were in private school and not competing for attention in overcrowded public schools like Chelsea would have to do when she started Pre-K.

"Can I ask you something personal?" Lyla said.

"Sure," Allison said, cringing inside.

"I know that you're mad at your mother right now, for telling your ex where you are, but, in general, was she a good parent?"

Allison wiped her mouth, then took a long drink of her mimosa.

"I wouldn't say she was a good parent. But I think she gets points that I made it to be an adult, alive and semi-well," she said.

They both looked sad.

"I'm sorry," Lyla said.

"What about other siblings?" Nova asked.

"Nope. Just us. And her never-ending, revolving door of boyfriends." Allison was embarrassed, but she didn't want to lie and paint a rosy childhood that never happened.

"Dad has never talked about her, but our mom has filled us in a little," Nova said. "I mean—about them. Not about you. We really didn't have any information about you, other than you existed out there somewhere."

Wow.

Allison didn't know what to think of that, but she wanted to change the trajectory of the conversation.

"Since we're getting personal," she asked, "does Nate have—"

"Nova? Lyla?"

Allison looked up to find a woman walking up the stairs from the riverside. She stopped at their table, all smiles.

"Mom," Lyla said. "What are you doing here?"

"Mom" pulled up a chair and sat down. "You must be Allison, dear. So nice to meet you. I'm Jan and these daughters of mine didn't tell me they were going to brunch today. Good thing I like to take my Sunday strolls at the river, or I'd have never seen you three sitting up here."

"We didn't think it—" Nova mumbled.

"—Exactly," Jan said curtly. "You didn't think."

Cue awkward silence before she turned her attention to Allison, "I've heard about your recent troubles. How are you doing? How are those precious children?"

"I—hello," Allison said. She should've known it was their mother. Jan and Lyla could be mistaken as sisters, they looked so much alike, other than Lyla dressed more like a boho princess and her mother like she was headed to the country club.

"I'm ... we're okay, I guess."

She didn't like that her business was being discussed.

Their server came by, and Jan asked for a glass, and ordered a Benedict with salmon, whatever that was. Then she turned back around.

"So, what's your plan? You staying in Tennessee?" she asked.

The girls looked nearly as uncomfortable as Allison felt.

I'm sorry, Lyla mouthed at her when their mom looked away.

Allison shrugged. It wasn't like they could help it. Jan looked like a nice enough person, and Allison didn't want things to be more awkward than they had to be, especially after the girls had given her such a wonderful day.

"I'm not sure, yet" Allison answered honestly.

"Nate never could man up and tell someone when they were being an imposition," Jan said. "So, you're probably safe to stay for at least a few months. Not sure if he has any savings to share with you, after spending so much on that land—and building that Godawful house. Considers himself some kind of Grizzly Adams, I think. Plans to retire there and live off the land. You probably should've caught up with him a few years ago when he wasn't broke."

Allison felt the heat climb up her neck, filling her cheeks. The woman obviously thought she was some kind of leech.

"Mom," Lyla said, "Did you hear about that woman on the Steam team?"

"What's the Steam team?" Nova asked.

Allison could see them working together to redirect the conversation.

"They're the women's fast-pitch team. Their first baseman is the extraordinary powerhouse, Kaylee Tow. They've nicknamed her 'grandma' because she's the only fifth-year player," Lyla said, laughing nervously.

Jan looked bored at Lyla's statement. She took a sip from Nova's glass and set it down, then smiled sympathetically. The gold bracelets on her wrist jingled loudly. "Back to Nate. I can't imagine how upset Sophia is," she said. "She's not used to not getting her way. I'm sure she's fit to be tied."

Nova moved her glass out of Jan's reach. "Mama!" she scolded. "What in the world is wrong with you?"

Jan looked astonished at her daughter's admonishment.

"Who is Sophia?" Allison asked.

Jan composed herself. "I'm sorry. I would've thought you'd have met her by now. That's Nate's girlfriend, though she tells people that she's his fiancée. She's been trying to seal the deal with him for more than two years. Just about had that ring, too, before you and the kids showed up. I've heard he put her off—for now—and she's not having it."

So, Nate did have a girlfriend. Allison figured it would be so. But now she felt guilty that he'd put his life on hold for her.

"Mom, do you know you sound like a jealous ex?" Lyla said.

Jan laughed dramatically. "No—believe me, if I wanted your father back, I'd have him. As a matter of fact, he tried to come back to me back in the day when he left your mother, Allison. Of course, I wasn't going to allow that. Once a cheater, always a cheater. Siren Sophia had better watch out."

"You don't even know her," Nova said.

"True, but, from afar, I think she's entertaining. She must be something. Nate is quite enamored by her most of the time. I'm sure he can't wait to get back to that little drama."

"Damn it, Mom. That's none of our business and definitely not any of yours. Where're you getting all this gossip from?" Lyla asked.

"Probably her devoted church group," Nova muttered. "That's what they call *asking for prayers* for someone, and then they spill the tea."

Jan tilted her head. "Not funny, Nova. I hear things from lots of places. Sophia has a reputation that hangs around like a black cloud, and everyone is taking bets on when she'll get him to the altar. Now that he's got three houseguests, maybe he's too tired to entertain Sophia and her notions. From what I've heard, she takes a lot of energy."

Lyla shook her head, visibly irritated. "We are changing the subject right *now*, Mom."

"Oh, did I say something wrong?" Jan said, looking at Allison innocently. "I'm sorry, Allison, if I made you uncomfortable. I'm sure Nate just loves having long lost relatives drop in and bring more excitement to his life. Girls, what did he have to promise you to get you to use your Sunday afternoon for Allison, and give him a break?"

They both glared at Jan.

Jan didn't seem ruffled. She fiddled with a huge diamond on her right hand. "Oh, and don't worry about Sophia. Nate is probably sneaking out and meeting her when you all are in bed. But, hey—what about those Atlanta Braves? You lived so close. Did you ever go see them play?"

CHAPTER 31

*I*t was at least another five days before Dom returned to the basement with fresh water. Lydia had resorted to drinking her wash water, but then that had run out, too. The only liquid she had left was her wastewater, and she'd rather die than resort to that. It would probably kill her anyway.

She'd gone the last two days without so much as a drop of food or water and had barely moved since the night before. This was the weakest she'd ever been, and it was like she could feel the life draining from her minute after minute.

Even Blackbird, staring at her from the window this morning, couldn't coax her to her feet. She talked to him from where she lay, though, thanking him for trying to keep her company.

It didn't even cause her to blink when the door suddenly opened, and Dom finally descended the stairs. She felt relief but didn't have the strength to turn and see him. She realized too late that she was holding her doll. There was no time to hide it now.

She jerked with fear when a parcel he threw landed after hitting her on the shoulders, then settling on the mattress in front of her face.

"Get dressed," he said.

When she slowly sat up, she saw that the parcel was simply a folded pair of jeans and a long-sleeved flannel shirt.

He tossed worn hiking boots down on the floor. A rolled-up sock fell out of one.

"You can get water once you've put the clothes on," he said. "You're coming upstairs."

Lydia's eyes widened.

Was she hallucinating? Did he say she was coming upstairs?

Maybe he wasn't even there.

She felt the flannel under her fingers. It was soft, feeling real.

"I guess you thought you were going to die down here before I got back," he said, his tone gloating. "There's been a lot going on outside, Lydia. Everything I've been telling you is about to come true. Started with one of America's biggest cell phone providers interrupting service on three carriers and millions of customers, then Facebook and Instagram going down for three hours yesterday. Not to mention the cyberattack on the United Airlines system that was compromised. That's what we call flexing. Someone is trying to get our attention."

Most of what he said went right over her head because Lydia was too depleted for logical thought. She needed water. And food.

But did it really matter anymore?

Should she just let go and finally be at peace?

She explored the edge of the shirt with her fingers, thinking. A long sleep sounded so tempting. She could watch over her children in a different way.

"Get up," he demanded, jolting her out of her thoughts of total abandon.

He wasn't going to go away.

She tried to stand, first getting to her knees before putting weight on one leg. She couldn't get the other one to cooperate and fell forward on the mattress, wobbling back up to her knees.

"I don't have time for this, Lydia," he said, coming to her side and pulling a key from his pocket. He quickly unlocked the chain around her ankle, then grabbed her under the arm, pulling her to her feet.

She felt like a rag doll as the room spun around her, making her nauseous.

"Damn it. Get yourself under control," he hissed. "We have things to do."

He put his arms under her legs and swung her up into his arms, then tossed her over his shoulder like a sack of potatoes. They'd only climbed one step on the stairwell when everything around her went black, and she faded into oblivion.

CHAPTER 32

$\mathcal{B}$y the time Allison and the kids arrived at the Best Western Motel on Lee Highway, she was as exhausted as they were. Thankfully, her Uber driver felt sorry for her and helped her get their bags all the way to the door of their room after she'd checked in.

Toby hadn't stirred the whole time. She thanked the heavens for having such a good baby. Unlike Chelsea had done, Toby rarely cried unless it was to signal something he needed like a diaper change, or a feeding.

A blast of cold air hit them as soon as she opened the door.

Allison lay Toby in the middle of one of the beds and made a pillow fort around him, then covered him with his blanket before going to the thermostat on the wall and turning down the air conditioning.

"Mommy, where are we?" Chelsea whined.

"It's another adventure, but, right now, it's time for bed. We'll talk tomorrow." She went to Chelsea next and pulled her clothes off and replaced them with her pajamas, then led her to the bed and tucked her in beside Toby.

"I miss Grandpa," Chelsea whined.

"I know." Allison tucked her elephant under the covers with her, next to her chest.

"Can I go swimming tomorrow?" she asked.

They'd passed the swimming pool outside on the way to their room.

"We'll see." Allison would have to see if it looked clean enough before making any promises.

Chelsea was too tired for much arguing, and she turned over and shut her eyes. Allison pulled the covers up and kissed her head, then went to the small desk and plugged her phone in.

They'd left Nate's house like thieves in the night, waiting until he'd gone to bed before sneaking out to the taxi that waited at the end of the driveway. She felt guilty for doing it, but he would've insisted they stay if he'd have known what she was planning.

That was her biggest problem, though.

Going to the other side of the bed, she sat down and took off her shoes, rubbing one foot as she considered their situation. She couldn't quite get a plan put together.

She had enough money to keep them at the motel for a few days but not enough for bus tickets back to Hart's Ridge. One option was calling around to try to get into a women's shelter in Chattanooga, but she really didn't want to do that. She could call Mabel, but then she and Taylor would have to know that things didn't work out with her dad, and that would be humiliating.

It wasn't as though they'd had an argument, or that Nate asked her to leave. Nothing like that had happened, but Allison didn't want to burden him any longer. Now he could go back to his life without the baggage of an extra daughter and grandkids weighing him down.

Lyla and Nova had tried to smooth over all the truths that Jan had told the weekend before, but they'd stuck with Allison and made her really think about things.

Why did she let herself think that after all the years of her father not trying to be in her life that he would want her now?

She might be desperate, but she was also proud. Too proud to force a relationship and her presence on someone who never wanted it in the first place. Nate was a gentleman and would never tell her she was an inconvenience. But that's exactly what she was now, and so many years before when he'd left them.

Anyway, Allison had been doing things on her own her entire adult life. Somehow, she'd figure it out. She always did.

She considered taking a shower but didn't feel comfortable leaving the kids alone, so she went to the bathroom and undressed. She washed down and slipped into a sleep shirt, brushed her teeth, and wiped down the countertop before going to sit on her side of the bed.

Even though she was exhausted, that didn't mean she'd be able to sleep. She stood and went to the window, peeking through the small gap in the curtains.

There was a man walking past the rooms, a cigarette in his hands. He looked angry in the dim light.

She closed the gap in the curtains and backed away, then took the chair from the small desk and carried it to the door. She wedged the top of it under the doorknob, checked the deadbolt one more time, and then went back to the bed to think of next steps.

Without transportation, every idea she had was quickly discarded.

If she got to Hart's Ridge, she could get her van from Taylor's farm. They could stay in the van for a while until she got another job. Her old babysitter would hopefully keep the kids while she worked, but she had to find something that paid as much as she'd made at Walmart, or she wouldn't be able to afford childcare and a place to live.

It had taken her two years to get to her salary there.

She thought of Wyatt.

If she could reach him, he'd be thrilled and would probably wire her some money through Western Union. She could get a ride to pick it up. But then he'd insist on seeing them when they got back to town.

Allison wasn't ready for that yet.

She thought of the van again and realized that if someone saw them staying in it and called it in, child services might take the kids.

Now she needed a job and an immediate place to live.

It seemed impossible. How did women start over all the time? Were they just smarter than her? Stronger? More resourceful? She wished she could go back in time. Do something different to change what had happened.

Her little house was so perfect, and the landlord had given her such a deal for rent. She'd never find that again, which meant they'd probably have to go back to an apartment complex where the rent was higher and the mix of people could be dangerous around the kids. She'd be scrambling from week to week to make ends meet. But that was the only thing she could think of. But she'd have to find the money for a deposit for the apartment. And the first month's rent.

Why was life so hard?

All she wanted was to raise her family in a nice but simple home, somewhere safe with a yard where she didn't have to worry about what her neighbors were doing, or someone strange coming up to the playground. Maybe have a dog.

She and Wyatt had it all at their fingertips, just within reach for a while. Then he had to screw it up. Now he had a warrant out for his arrest and, if he even showed his face in Hart County, he was going to jail.

Toby's father was going to be a felon.

It was bad enough that he had a problem with his temper and didn't think twice about using his hands on her, but now he was going to have a record. He'd probably lost his job, too.

Why did she pick such bad men? Was she just like her mother, always running away from good ones and right into the arms of those who would treat her poorly? Was she living some sort of generational cycle, and this was going to be her destiny?

To always be heartbroken and lonely?

Damn it, she didn't want to be her mother!

It infuriated her when she felt a tear fall from the corner of her eye, drop onto her nose, and then roll off onto the pillow.

She wiped at it angrily. She needed to be strong. Chelsea and Toby depended on her, and she couldn't be weak or let herself drown in a pity party.

Lucy came to mind. Taylor's sister had gone from pregnant and homeless to being her own boss and building a career that would make her and her son comfortable for years to come. How had Lucy figured out that she could even do anything in the art arena?

And Jo. She was raising Levi without help of anyone. Sure, she had a job with the family business but, from what Allison had heard, Jo had done well before that, always finding a way to come out on top, despite being a single parent. She also had talents in the art world. A different arena than Lucy, but something she could do if she felt like leaving the farm to go out on her own.

And Lyla. She was another great example of someone who had a dream and went for it. Her salon was on prime property, right downtown. Her rent must cost a fortune, but it appeared that she could afford it easily.

Allison didn't have any talents that she knew of. She could unload a truck, stock shelves, and run a register like nobody's business. Well, she also kept up with what needed to be ordered for the paper goods department and had gotten great at balancing the lead times with shipments so that she never had too much stock but was able to get her orders there right on time. She was also great at picking popular items with low cost but high markups for her displays.

The store manager had told her he was going to be giving her a bigger department soon, and that was supposed to come with another raise.

Allison didn't mind a career in retail, though she still wondered what else was out there that she might possibly be able to do. Something that paid more, with less hours or time on her feet. She wasn't always going to be young and energetic. Well, she wasn't actually energetic most days now, especially with so much stress on her shoulders all the time.

Dreams were not something she'd ever had the time to think about. Even if she knew something to dream for, she was too busy just surviving to reach out and try to grab one.

The morning was coming soon, so Allison forced her eyes shut. Her head was too busy to come up with a plan tonight, anyway.

Yes, tomorrow.

She'd figure out something.

She always did.

CHAPTER 33

*A*llison laughed as she leaned over the side of the bathtub, washing Toby's tiny feet while he kicked with glee. He loved the water and his big sister, and, with her in the tub with him, he was tickled pink.

They were on day three at the motel, and Allison's mom had promised her that on Friday she'd send her enough money to get them bus tickets home. That was the least she could do, but, if she was able to pull it off, Allison would be surprised.

She'd texted Nate and told him that she appreciated his kindness, but that she and the kids were going to make their own way. She'd ignored his multiple responses asking where she was, and his pleas to come back.

It was better this way. Break it up before she got too attached to him

Her plan was to go back to Hart's Ridge and stay with her mom just for a few days, and, if things were still not coming together, she'd call Mabel and ask to come back. Her mom was begging for a chance to make things right, so Allison was going to give it to her. She'd also said she was working on a surprise.

The thought of going there made her very nervous, but they didn't have many options. Once there, she'd go to Walmart and try to get her job back. Then talk to the babysitter.

Lastly, pray that she could find them somewhere affordable to live.

At least she was doing something and not letting the doubt creep in and paralyze her. One step was better than doing nothing.

A knock on the door startled her, and she glanced anxiously toward it, half expecting trouble before remembering that she'd called and asked for more clean towels to be brought to the room.

"Mommy, who's there?" Chelsea's voice piped up from the bath. "Pizza?"

Nate had ordered pizza several times in the last few weeks and now Chelsea expected every knock on the door was a delivery of her favorite food.

"No, it's just towels." Allison replied. "Stay in the tub for a minute, okay? Mommy will be right back."

She wrapped Toby up and approached the door with him in her arms. She didn't know why they didn't just leave the towels out there instead of interrupting her. When she opened the door, she jumped.

Wyatt stood on the other side. He leaned against the door-frame, his foot as a stopper, blocking her from shutting him out. He held a brown bag with the neck of a liquor bottle sticking out of it. He smiled at her and Allison's stomach twisted into knots.

"Wyatt, what are you doing here?" she asked, her voice strained. He looked like shit, his clothes rumpled and his eyes red-rimmed. He was pale, like he'd been sick.

She looked over and around him, hoping for someone there to signal. For once, no one else was out and about.

"I needed to see you, Allison," he said, serious now with his eyes pleading. "I've been thinking a lot about us, about everything I've done wrong. I want to make things right."

"How did you know that we were here?"

"How do you think? Your mom cannot keep a secret. She's also a hopeless romantic and urged me to come."

Allison's jaw clenched as she struggled to contain her anger. This had to be her mother's *surprise she said she was working on.* Allison wanted to scream, to tell him to leave and never come back. But she couldn't risk escalating the situation, not with her kids right there in the room.

From the bathroom she heard Chelsea singing a song as she splashed.

"You know there's a warrant for your arrest," Allison whispered. "What if someone sees you? They'll take you straight in and lock you up."

"That's why you need to let me come in. You don't really want me to go to jail, do you?"

The question sounded loaded, as though her answer might trigger something terrible.

"No, but listen, Wyatt," she said, forcing herself to remain calm. "I appreciate that you want to talk, but now's not a good time. I have to get Chelsea out of the bath, and—"

"Let me help," Wyatt interrupted, pushing his way past her into the room and letting the door close behind him. "I can take Toby while you finish up with her."

Allison's heart raced as Wyatt took Toby from her arms, her instincts screaming at her to protect her children. But she knew she had to tread carefully, to keep Wyatt calm until she could figure out a way to get rid of him. "Okay, fine," she said through gritted teeth, her mind racing. "But just give me a minute, alright? I'll be right back."

What do I do? Who do I call?

Her mind was flooded with questions, then she realized that her phone was on the bed where Wyatt had gone to sit with Toby.

Panic surged through her. She was cut off from the outside world, completely at his mercy.

She hurried into the bathroom.

"Chelsea, your daddy is here," she said.

Her daughter lit up. As far as Chelsea was concerned, Wyatt was the only father she knew. Children forgave easily and she didn't seem to recall the last night she'd seen Wyatt. The night it all fell apart and she'd left with her bruised and swollen mother.

"Yay!" Chelsea said, standing up and slapping water from her arms.

"Let me dry and dress you first." Allison worked quickly, afraid that Wyatt might leave with Toby. She thought murderous thoughts while she worked and, when Chelsea was ready, Allison took a deep breath.

She pushed aside her fear and they returned to the main room.

"Daddy!" Chelsea yelled, running to his side. He gave her a hug with the arm that wasn't holding his son.

"Hello, Sunshine," he said, giving Allison a triumphant grin.

How quickly he forgot what he'd done to his sunshine's bedroom.

"Okay, Wyatt," Allison said, trying to sound casual. "Give me Toby. Let's talk."

She turned cartoons on the television for Chelsea and as Wyatt launched into his apologies and promises, Allison listened with half an ear as she eyed her phone under his arm. She fed Toby a bottle and her mind raced with thoughts of escape. She thought of the moves that Nate had shown her, but every scenario that she conjured up had her struggling to grab both children in an escape.

As the hours dragged on, and both the kids went to sleep, Wyatt grew drunker and more belligerent, and Allison's hopes of a peaceful resolution faded. She watched in dismay as he ranted and raved, blaming her for everything that had gone wrong in his life.

Finally, his drunken ramblings dwindled into soft snores, and Allison saw her chance. She began to quietly gather their belongings, her hands shaking as she packed their things into bags.

She went to the bed and slowly pulled her phone away from where it sat next to Wyatt's sleeping form. She stood there and shot off a text, hoping that the recipient would see it.

Carefully, she picked up Toby, holding him close to her chest.

But just as she started to turn to Chelsea, Wyatt stirred, his eyes snapping open with a dangerous glint.

"Where do you think you're going, Allison?" he slurred, his voice thick with anger.

Her heart pounded in her chest.

"Please, Wyatt, let us go," she pleaded, her voice trembling.

His eyes flashed with rage, and, before Allison could react, he grabbed her wrist and twisted it until she let go of her phone. He slipped it into his pocket as she struggled to hold Toby with one arm.

"You're a whore and a liar," he said, his voice low and threatening. "Got a boyfriend, don't you? Trying to sneak out to him, huh? You ain't going nowhere but to bed."

With a shove, he herded her toward the bed, his hands rough and unyielding. Then he shoved her onto it and walked away.

Tears welled in Allison's eyes as she huddled with Chelsea and Toby, her mind racing with fear and uncertainty. She knew she had to stay strong for her children, but the weight of the situation pressed down on her like a leaden blanket.

Desperately, she searched for a glimmer of hope, a way to escape the nightmare that had engulfed them. And, as exhaustion finally claimed her, she prayed that when the sun came up, he would leave.

WHEN ALLISON WAS AWAKENED, it was by a gentle shake on her shoulder. Confusion clouded her mind as she blinked away the remnants of sleep, trying to make sense of her surroundings. But when she looked around the hotel room, the silence echoed like a cavernous void.

"Chelsea?" she called out, her voice tinged with uncertainty.

And then, like a beacon in the darkness, her sisters appeared in the doorway, their faces drawn with concern.

"We're here, Allison," Nova said softly, her voice filled with reassurance. "Everything's going to be okay."

Allison sat straight up in bed, frantic to lay eyes on her kids. She saw Chelsea then, on the other bed, busy coloring in a book.

Lyla held Toby. He was awake and alert.

"Where's Wyatt?" Allison asked.

"He's in custody," Nova whispered, glancing at Chelsea. "Dad got your message last night and we've been here, waiting with the police until one of you opened the door. Dad wouldn't let them break it down or cause a scene, because of the kids."

"But they listened at the door to make sure he wasn't hurting you," Lyla said. "As expected, he eventually came outside to get something from the old car he drove up here. They grabbed him as soon as the door shut behind him."

Allison's heart swelled with gratitude as she listened to their words, tears of relief streaming down her cheeks. They'd been out there all night, making sure she and the kids were still safe. And the best news was that Wyatt was in custody and her children wouldn't have more trauma from the take down.

Lyla pulled the covers back off Allison. "Now pack your stuff, little sister. Dad said you're coming home whether you want to or not. He's sitting outside by the door. He wanted to let you sleep until things simmered down again, but I think they're all gone."

Nova had gone to the window and peeked out.

"Yep. Coast is clear. Let's hit it."

Allison's breath caught in her throat as she absorbed their words, overwhelmed by their concern. In her darkest moment, her family had come through for her, and that was something she'd never had happen in her life. She truly didn't know what to make of it, but she was grateful.

CHAPTER 34

$\mathcal{T}$aylor was starting to feel carsick by the time they'd driven round and round and up the mountain. They arrived at a farm gate that marked the entrance to a property that, on paper, belonged to a dead man. She had to admit, though, it was gorgeous scenery at the top. Only twelve miles from downtown Ellijay, but, once they passed the subdivision and climbed higher up the mountain, it felt like they were in the middle of nowhere.

Diesel panted.

"I'll get you some water when we stop, boy," she said, patting his head.

The old listing for 301 Cohutta Wilderness Trail said it was a private mountain home with over 14 acres of land bordered by 20,000 acres of national forest. It bragged of panoramic views of the Cohutta Wilderness and wildlife, complete with hiking and biking trails and endless hunting and fishing in the nearby Mountain Town Creek.

Sam had looked at it with her and said it sounded like a bachelor's dream. Taylor hoped he wasn't thinking of becoming a bachelor again and told him as much before he'd grinned and enveloped her in a big hug.

"Why do you think this property wasn't part of the estate that the wife got?" Caleb asked. "Or what was left of it after the big loss?"

"I'm not sure, but Norman's name wasn't anywhere in the paperwork I found at the courthouse," Taylor said. "He's never been an owner."

"Maybe she didn't want it. If Norman was attached to it in any way, even emotionally, she probably wouldn't touch it."

Taylor opened the truck door and Diesel couldn't wait. He leaped over her lap and jumped down, immediately going to some bushes, and retching up his breakfast. Then he turned and looked fine, a light in his eyes as though to say, *c'mon ... let's go ... I'm good now ...*

"Okay, so you're not into driving up mountains but you like it when we get here," Taylor said. "Noted."

She and Caleb got out and went to the gate. It had a huge tractor chain and padlock around it.

"You got anything in the truck to cut that?" Caleb asked.

"Nope."

"I guess we walk," he said, then climbed over and held a hand to help her.

"Let me get something first," Taylor said. She went to her truck and got out a can of bear spray and hooked it on her belt before climbing over the gate.

Diesel squirmed through the bars, joining her on the other side.

"Good call," Caleb said when he saw the can. "Did you ever see a picture of that bear that Danny Hall took down around here a few years ago?"

"Nope. Never heard of him."

"Five hundred and fifteen pounds and shot it with a bow. Took seven men to drag it out."

"Jeez. Hope we don't see any." She joined him on the other side, glad it wasn't bear hunting season. She didn't feel like looking out for passing arrows—or an errant bullet.

This search was their final lead and was going to be the dead end of the case if they found nothing. She'd had a long talk with Caleb after he'd told her about the blowup at home with Grace. It took some convincing, but he'd agree that after this, he'd stop obsessing over Lydia, and go get some professional help.

Taylor felt a little guilty for getting his hopes up. If she hadn't gone back to Mabel and asked who the arresting officer was when Gwen Kelley had come to the shelter, they wouldn't know a thing about the connection. She'd thought about not telling him, and investigating it herself, but, if he'd ever found out, he wouldn't forgive her. He had to know that he'd followed every lead to the very end himself, if he was ever going to be able to let it go.

"Any news on the girl?" Caleb asked.

"Jill Kelley? Not as of this morning. I caught the latest press conference on the way out. Her mom has stopped giving statements and has a family rep now."

"I feel for her. No one can imagine the pain of someone you love going missing unless it happens to them."

They walked half a mile and, strangely, came to another farm gate. It looked much newer than the one at the foot of the driveway.

"Someone is really into security against vehicles," Caleb said. "Or they're raising some high dollar goats on this mountain."

It was secured with another chain and padlock, so they climbed over again. For this gate, Caleb had to hoist Diesel over to Taylor.

As they walked, covering one acre at a time, they talked, touching on several subjects before it came back round to Caleb's home situation and his agreement to let his sister-in-law move in.

"I don't know why I was so resistant," he said. "Blair keeps things running smoothly and her help with Zoey is invaluable."

"I'm sure that it feels like she's taking Lydia's place sometimes," Taylor said. "But you must put the well-being of the girls over your feelings. I think you know that I basically raised my sisters when we were growing up."

He nodded. "I've picked up on some of your past."

Taylor wondered who had been talking at the department. She hated gossip.

"Well, I can tell you," she said, "if we would've had someone step in when my mom was taken from us as kids, our life would've been so much easier. My dad had some girlfriends, but they were few and far between and never lasted because of his drinking."

"How's he doing now with that?" Caleb stepped over a fallen tree then turned to give his hand.

Taylor took it, to be nice.

"He's not drinking but it's a one-day-at-time kind of thing. He's not secure in his sobriety, and he struggles. I think that the engagement of my mom and Ellis last year set him back. But I was proud of him for being at the wedding. Thankfully, he's let Cecil back into his life and calls on him when he's feeling weak."

"Still holds that torch for Cate, huh?"

"Yeah. I wish he'd find someone who makes him happy enough that he'd let it go."

"Deep love isn't like that, Taylor," Caleb said quietly. "No one could ever replace Lydia, no matter how wonderful they might be."

"I get that, and I think you can't look at it as a replacement. If someone you like comes along, you should look at it as a bonus love. You were blessed to have the first love story, and then—sometimes—when that one ends, you get one more. I do believe that a person can have more than one great love in their life."

She wasn't speaking from experience, as Sam was the only

man she'd ever fallen in true love with, but she hoped that Caleb was taking in some of what she said. If this was the last lead for Lydia, it was time for him to move on.

"Damn, how far into this property is the house?" Caleb asked.

"I looked at the aerial map for it and it looked like it was in the middle. I think we have a few acres to go." They were still on the driveway, though the further they went in, the more grown up the weeds were, nearly hiding it. None of the land looked maintained and she wondered if it would be the same around the house. If no one had lived there in the years since Norman's brother died, the place was probably ramshackle.

"Subject change, then. How's Jo doing?" Caleb asked. "She's really been through it, hasn't she?"

That was an understatement. Jo still felt responsible for what had happened at the farm, at the hands of Eldon, a man she'd brought in among them.

"She's doing okay, I guess," Taylor said. "It's better now that Cate has recovered and is back to working full time. Jo felt so guilty about her getting shot that she hibernated for a while, not coming out of her cabin unless it was for work. She won't talk about the incident, so we don't bring it up."

"What about the community theatre? Did she ever go back?"

"No. She won't talk about that either. I wish she'd not let what happened ruin the one thing that made her so happy. When she was working there, she was full of energy. Always smiling. Eldon messed that up for her. Now she focuses on her work at the farm, and whatever Levi is up to."

"She's a good mom, isn't she?"

"The best. I can only hope that, if I ever have a child, I can be half the mom my sisters are to their children. Even Lucy—the wildest of us Gray girls—has turned out to be something none of us expected. Not only with Johnny, but she's killing it in her career." Taylor stopped for a minute to get her breath.

"You okay?" Caleb asked, pausing with her.

"Should've brought water," she replied, though she wasn't sure if even water would've helped. For some reason, she'd been feeling a bit out of sorts over the last few days, but it was probably exhaustion. Or stress, without a doubt.

They started again, then rounded a bend in the driveway. The house came into view.

"Finally," she said, breathing a sigh of relief. Now they just had to walk all the way back. When they finished looking around, she was going to sit down for a bit. The map she'd seen of the place showed a creek near the house, and she planned to find it.

Diesel followed some sort of scent trail up to the porch, his thirst forgotten with the array of scents around the place.

"Diesel, come back," Taylor said, then worried someone might see him and do something stupid.

"I think he's fine. Doesn't look like anyone is at home," Caleb said. "If he was here, there'd be some kind of transportation out here. I don't see any."

There wasn't a garage, only a carport with trash cans stacked at the back and a rusty chain on the ground that looked like a dog had been attached to it.

She looked at the house again. For a second home, it was just the right size for a small family. The listing said just under two thousand square feet, but with the tall slope of the roof, it appeared bigger.

It wasn't quite ramshackle, but you also couldn't say it was well kept. She noticed that one of the steps leading up to the porch was recently replaced, but the few flowerpots lined up on the top railing sported nothing but dry dirt and some blackened stems.

"Looks like no one has bothered with spring cleaning in some time," Caleb said, pointing to the pile of leaves that looked blown by the wind into the far corner.

Taylor went to the window, but heavy drapes covered every inch of the view inside. The door had a pane at the top, and she stood on her toes to look, but someone had put a dark film over it.

Caleb knocked loudly, then called out. "Anyone in there?"

No one answered.

"Let's go around back," Taylor said. Diesel had already left them, but he wouldn't go far without her. Still yet, she kept an eye out for him and, when she heard him rustling around in the woods next to the house, she continued to the back.

"Nice spot," Caleb said when they came around the corner to be met with a big back porch that looked out over the mountains.

They went up there and Taylor saw that the French doors were covered, hiding their view inside from there, too. She turned and looked out over the backyard. It was completely wooded, but the height of the deck made it possible to see for miles in the distance, looking over the national forest.

"So, this is what it looks like from an elevation of 2400 feet," she said.

"Gorgeous," Caleb murmured. "I could live out here in this quiet and solitude."

Conk-la-ree, conk-la-ree ...

Taylor heard the call of a bird in the sky. Seeing a blackbird soaring above her, she recalled seeing one before on an earlier visit to this area, wondering of its significance.

Diesel paid no heed to the blackbird's plaintive call. He instead stood at the bottom of a big oak tree, looking up as a small rodent ran up its bark.

"Look at that," Caleb exclaimed. "A squirrel without a tail. Never seen one before."

"I guess Diesel hasn't either. He's waiting for it to come back down."

Then Taylor heard water trickling just beyond the densest of the trees and knew that was most likely the creek. Diesel must've heard it, too, for he gave up on the squirrel and bolted in that direction.

"He's going after a drink," she said when Caleb seemed startled.

"I'm going to meet him there in a minute myself."

"Same." On the ground was a fire-pit, with four black Adirondack chairs set around it. Taylor went over and looked in the pit.

"Someone has been here. There's been a fire not too long ago," she said. Inside the metal ring were ashes and remnants of kindling. It was dry, and Taylor knew that the area had gotten quite a thunderstorm not two weeks before.

Caleb had gone to peek inside an outbuilding, and he covered the distance quickly back to Taylor, and looked with her. He nodded in agreement, then went back to the house and began walking around it to the opposite corner from where they'd come.

Within seconds, he shouted at her to come.

Taylor ran to where he crouched at the corner closest to them. There was a window at ground level and Caleb was kneeling, looking inside.

"There's a mattress on the floor," he said, his face next to the glass as he used his hands to shield the glare.

Taylor dropped to her knees beside him. There wasn't much room to look because it appeared that someone had used a black crayon to draw a bird on the inside of the panes. It was very well drawn and looked eerily realistic.

Caleb moved, giving the space up for Taylor to look. It wasn't a big room at all. Maybe the size of her bathroom at home. In it, she saw the old mattress lying on the concrete floor. And there were two buckets—one in one area of the room, and the other on the far side. In the middle was an area rug as the only spot of color, but, other than a homemade broom, nothing much else to make the room look livable.

"I want to get in that house," Caleb said, suddenly more alert and determined.

"You know we can't. No search warrant," she warned. "The

FBI was probably already here, anyway, Caleb." She could feel his sudden excitement and didn't want him to take it too far just to have the hope dashed.

"Not if they didn't know about this place." He jumped up and finished scoping out the other sides of the home.

She continued to look through the basement window, zoning in on the room, inch by inch, now in detective mode. She could see the last few steps of a stairwell leading up. They weren't dusty at all.

There was also a large piece of furniture on the left wall. Some kind of antique cabinet people used as closets long ago. Taylor wondered what it held.

Secrets of Kenneth Addler? Or from Norman Addler?

When the clouds above her broke, a tiny sliver of light shone on the glass and Taylor felt her gaze pulled back to the previously dark area of stairwell. What she saw now caused a tingling sensation to start in her feet and work its way up her body, landing most evident in her wrists as she still held them up to the window, framing her view inside.

On the bottom step she could see something. The ray of light hit it just right and it sparkled, glinting in the sudden sun.

She couldn't tell the shape of it from her distance away, but she knew one thing ...

It was an earring.

CHAPTER 35

$\mathcal{C}$aleb's shoulders sagged with relief when he saw the sheriff's truck come rattling up to the house. He'd obviously brought a heavy-duty bolt cutter with him, so he didn't have to take the long hike like the rest of the team who was already there, waiting on the search warrant.

Four hours was a long time to sit and worry. But, in the world of search warrants, having one signed by the judge in just four hours was a miracle. That was a silver lining to small towns. They were able to cut through a lot of the red tape usually needed for a legal search and seize.

"Sheriff said I owe him a big one for this," Taylor said. "I hope we have something here."

"We do," Caleb said. "I feel it."

The sheriff pulled up behind the other cars and parked and got out. He whistled, waving at the guys to come in and listen. Caleb and Taylor walked over. Penner, Kuno, and a few of their part-timers gathered close, too.

Sheriff held a pry bar in his hand.

"Detective Weaver has been called home on a family emergency. I need to remind you all that this could possibly be a crime scene, so don't go stomping all over the property. Only myself, Gray, and Grimes will go in," he said. "If we find anything at all that tells us Lydia Grimes was ever here, I'm calling the FBI. If we don't find any evidence, then this whole escapade goes no further, and that includes talking about it to your families. I don't want our department to be the laughingstock of the county for chasing a whim."

Caleb nodded respectfully, but—in his gut—he wasn't too happy with the sheriff. If it was his wife, damn straight he'd also continue to look for evidence that she was dead, and he wouldn't be calling it a whim.

He felt Taylor squeeze his arm, a silent reminder to just let it slide and focus on the task at hand, and he stepped in line behind her. Sheriff led the way but stood aside and handed Caleb the pry bar.

"Don't be too hard on it. You'll have to repair it yourself if this turns into nothing. I don't have the budget for a handyman."

Caleb nodded. It only took him a minute before the door was easily separated from the frame with minimal splintering. He stood to the side and let Taylor go first, then the sheriff before he cautiously stepped into the foyer.

The sheriff pointed each of them in a direction and Caleb took his, swinging his gun first around every corner until he'd cleared all the rooms on his side.

"Clear!" Taylor called out a few times before meeting the guys in the living room.

They put their guns away and took more time to look around.

They were standing in the living room of an open-concept cabin with a peaked ceiling laden with thick, rustic beams.

Their senses were immediately assaulted by the musty smell of neglect, though there was nothing visibly out of order. It just smelled unlived in. The interior was dimly lit, with heavy drapes covering the windows, casting long shadows across the worn, wooden floors. There was no television, and, other than an old leather couch and chair, a stereo system with stacks of CDs taking up one wall was about all that was in evidence.

Sheriff Dawkins went to the windows along the front and yanked open the curtains, spilling light into the big room, finding little more.

The living room was sparsely furnished, with a faded couch and a coffee table littered with old Wall Street Journal magazines. Caleb's eyes scanned the room, noting the absence of personal touches or family photos. It felt cold and impersonal, like a shell of a home rather than a place where someone lived.

"Stay alert," Taylor muttered to Caleb as they moved deeper into the house. "Keep an eye out for anything suspicious."

Caleb nodded.

As they entered the kitchen, his gaze fell upon stacks of canned food on the counter—tuna, beans, and soups—all neatly arranged as if someone had meticulously stocked up for an apocalypse.

In the corner of the room, Caleb spotted a set of pet bowls on the floor.

"Let's split up and search the bedrooms," Caleb suggested, his voice low with unease. "I'll take the upstairs; you check down here."

Taylor headed down the hallway toward the bedrooms. Caleb ascended the creaky staircase, the wood groaning under his weight with each step.

The upstairs bedrooms were just as barren as the rest of the house—barely made up mattresses on metal frames, dresser tops devoid of any personal items. But, as Caleb rummaged through the drawers, his fingers brushed against something cold and metallic—a knife hidden away among the clothes.

His heart raced as he pocketed the knife, his mind racing with possibilities. What kind of person kept a weapon like that in their bedroom?

Descending the stairs, Caleb rejoined Taylor in the kitchen, his eyes scanning the room for any signs of disturbance. That's when Taylor called out, her voice tinged with excitement.

"Hey, come take a look at this!"

Hurrying over to the island, Caleb saw Taylor leaning over a notebook left behind on the counter. She pointed to a note scribbled on Friday of the next week.

"Norman has been here," she said.

Caleb looked. The note read,

Friday, March 3rd—Deposition

"Yep, looks like he's been coming here," Sheriff Dawkins said. "But we've secured the house and found nothing. I'm going outside."

"We haven't found the basement yet," Caleb said. "That's where the earring is."

Taylor nodded in agreement. "But what I want to know is how do you get down there? We've checked every corner up here. Did we miss an outside entrance?"

"I'll go out and look for myself," Sheriff said.

He left them standing in the kitchen and they heard the storm door slam.

Suddenly, Taylor leaned too heavily on the island counter, and it shifted beneath her.

"What do we have here?" she said, looking down to see wheels underneath.

"Wait—that sneaky son of a—" he pushed the island aside, revealing a hidden door in the floor. "Now we're getting somewhere." Heart pounding with anticipation, he knelt and opened the hatch, revealing the stairwell to the basement below.

He looked up at Taylor. She was the unspoken lead.

"You go first," she said.

Caleb drew his gun.

Slowly and quietly, he descended into the dim room, Taylor right behind him.

At the bottom of the stairs, they were met with a sight more chilling than it had looked through the window. It was a small, makeshift living space, complete with a thin mattress on the floor and a few buckets. The first one was empty. Taylor went to the other one in the corner and pulled the piece of fabric off the top, then cringed.

"Makeshift toilet," she said.

Taylor spotted something that looked like a poorly put-together rag doll lying on the mattress near the wall. It's face was drawn on crudely, the mouth either a half smile or frown, too hard to tell.

The only saving grace of the bland area was a colorful rug on the floor, and some artwork drawn on the concrete wall with what appeared to be crayons. It was of an ivy plant that started from a crack in the floor, then snaked up the wall, its leaves getting fuller and brighter the closer they climbed toward the light. An outline of a leaf started at the top but wasn't finished. The drawing was in the same style as the blackbird drawn on the glass. On another wall, someone had used crayons to draw twisted, distorted black figures—a macabre display of madness and despair.

Next to an empty gallon milk jug, two crayons lay smashed in the floor, the black and green crumbles mixed into a smear of dark green, a color imagined that the forest looked like at night.

It was clear that someone had been living here, hiding away from the world above, and using the crayons to pass time.

"Why would he stay down here?" Caleb asked.

"I don't think he would," Taylor said. "You forgot about this."

She bent at the last stair and picked up the earring.

Caleb's hands trembled as he reached out to touch it, his mind reeling with the implications. Could it be a coincidence? Not to him, but would the sheriff try to paint it as such?

He looked around the room, staring at the drawings again. He was suddenly hit with a memory of all the old sketch pads that Lydia kept in the attic, drawings from her high school years when she'd dreamed of being an artist. A gift she'd put away because she "didn't have time for hobbies," she'd said the one time he'd asked her about it.

The drawings here contradicted each other. To Caleb, the vine portrayed hope in its reach for the sun and the improvement of its detail and color as it went higher and higher. The bird on the window felt like a symbol of protection, a connection to the outside.

He turned back to the darker drawings. They portrayed misery and a feeling of being lost, but one figure on the wall stood out more than others. It was a female, and a bird stood on the woman's shoulder.

Lydia had drawn them all. Caleb knew it more than he'd ever known anything in his life. His wife had been here, and not just for a short period.

"You're right, Taylor," he said. "He didn't stay down here in this hell hole. Lydia did. Go tell Sheriff to call the feds. We've got a crime scene."

He said a silent prayer, thankful that the search for Lydia hadn't ended. Then he squared his shoulders and took a deep breath.

A whole new journey was about to begin.

CHAPTER 36

*N*ate sat down on the end of the bed and put his head in his hands. Allison waited him out, knowing, if she spoke now, he'd back down from whatever it was he wanted to say.

It felt good to be back at his house. Comfortable, like an old pair of slippers.

She'd just hung up the phone with Deputy Gray and filled her in on everything that had happened. Wyatt was in jail, pending bond. Taylor let her know that Wyatt would be transported to Hart County to face his charges there, once Tennessee was done with him. She'd sounded relieved that at least that part of Allison's ordeal was over, and she could stop hiding.

Especially because Allison had called while Taylor was on day two of a big case, and camping out at the crime scene. One that she whispered was now swarming with search teams and agencies like the FBI after they'd found a lead on a previously closed case.

Taylor was going to be busy for a while.

To Allison, it sounded like a new saga, rather than an old case, and she wondered if it was related to anyone she knew from Hart's Ridge.

Nate finally looked up, but not at her. He kept his eyes trained on the television instead of looking at her.

"I think—to make you understand things—I need to start at the beginning," he said. "It's a cliché, but I met your mom at a bar."

"And you left Jan and the girls for her."

He shook his head. "No. Jan and I had divorced more than a year before that when I turned down a promotion. I couldn't be the behind-the-desk man she wanted me to become. I told her I'd always be a lineman, out in the open and not confined by walls and a time clock. Jan wanted the country club scene—bright lights and champagne—and I was happy with campfires and beer. We were never a good match."

Allison could see that. Nate was born to be a blue-collar worker and was proud of it. Jan was—well, not the type of woman to settle for that.

"Your mom and I hit it off immediately. Opposites attract and all that. She was the life of the party, and I was the guy who liked to sit quietly in the corner. With her, I felt more alive than I ever had. Long story short, we were married four months later. You came six months after that, though I swear I didn't marry her just because she was pregnant. I loved her wild streak and thought that having you would tame it just enough that she'd settle down and be a good wife and mother."

Allison thought of last Christmas when her mother had shown up drunk to go with her to take Chelsea to see Santa at the mall. Her mom had insisted on sitting on Santa's lap, too, and other adults in line had turned away, giving Allison some privacy during her humiliation.

Nate glanced at her, then back at the television. "When you were three years old, I had to go out of town for a four-day training seminar. On day two, I came down with something and they didn't want me spreading it around, so they told me to go home. I took the red-eye and used my key to let myself in. It was close to midnight, so I set my things down and went upstairs. Opened the door and I guess you could say she was creating her own little late show with a man she'd met at the gym."

Allison couldn't imagine that her mother had ever gone to a gym.

She also couldn't imagine why that was her train of thought.

"I wanted to hurt them both, but I didn't. I did nothing other than back out of the room. She chased me down and swore it was the first time, that it was nothing. I forgave her, but I didn't forget. Two months later, I ran into the same guy. He apologized and told me he wasn't the first or the last. When I confronted your mother, she blamed me. Said my job took me away and she was lonely."

"Sounds about like her," Allison said. Her mother changed boyfriends nearly as much as she changed underwear. Even now, her wild streak was anything but tamed.

"I asked her what she wanted to do, and she said she wanted to be free. I told her to go ahead and have her fun, but to leave you with me. She refused, obviously. I tried to fight her in court but, back then, you had to have a lot of dirt on a woman to take their child from them. She got custody, I got child support, and then six months later she left town with some bozo."

"You decided it was too much trouble to keep up with her," Allison said.

He turned to look at her. "No, that's not what I decided. I tried to find her, and sometimes I would, in the beginning. But she'd take off again, no forwarding address."

"What about the child support?" Allison couldn't imagine her mother not claiming the money.

Nate shrugged. "She'd decided by then that it was more fun to taunt me by not letting me see my kid. She told lies on me. Said I was a horrible father and she had to keep you away from me.

That I was dangerous. People told me what she said. It always got back to me how she continued to try to paint herself as a victim. She got more from her men that way. Your mom was a very pretty woman and her damsel in distress act probably brought her more than I could ever give her."

"She still plays victim," Allison said. "Every mess she makes she blames on someone else. And she's not so pretty anymore. Her late nights drinking has taken a toll."

He looked sad. "I'm sorry about that, Allison. I can only tell you that she has her own demons. She didn't have the best childhood."

"Neither did I."

"And I'm even sorrier about that."

Allison didn't know what to think about his story. Was it even possible that her mother couldn't have been tracked down? Had Nate tried hard enough?

"I'll admit that when you turned about twelve, I stopped trying to find her. Stopped trying to find you. I imagined that she'd finally settled down, married, and that she'd just run again if I found you. I decided that I didn't want to hurt anymore, Allison. I couldn't keep it up. It was killing me. I had to let you go."

"You talk about your hurt," she said. "And mom talks about hers. But what about mine? Why don't my parents ever think about my pain?"

He looked stricken. "I thought about your hurt all the time! But when my letters continued to come back to me, unopened and undeliverable at every address I could find online, I convinced myself you didn't want to read them. That it wasn't just her anymore, that you didn't want me either."

Allison shook her head, feeling angry.

"I was wrong. I know that, now. These last weeks of getting to know you have been some of the best weeks I've ever had. You have brought so much sunshine into my life. You—and Chelsea. Toby. I can't wait to get home from work just because I knew all of you were here, waiting. When I found you gone, I thought I'd lose my mind. And when you called, and were in trouble, it scared me to death."

She swallowed the lump in her throat.

"I'll be right back," he said, then left the room quietly.

Toby stirred in his sleep and Allison rubbed his back until he was motionless again. She would never, ever leave him. Or Chelsea. If someone took them, she'd never give up finding them. She would also never keep their fathers from seeing them if they cleaned up their acts and behaved responsibly. A relationship between a child and their father wasn't the mother's choice—and they should never have all the power.

Nate returned and set a boot box on the bed near her.

"You might not want them, but I kept them in the hopes that one day you'd grow up and come looking for me."

She lifted the lid.

Inside were stacks of letters and postcards, all with her name on them.

Unopened and stamped *not at this address* in red.

The tears came now, and Allison rubbed at her face. All her life she'd thought her father had forgotten her.

"Do you want to read them?" he asked. "Then maybe you'll believe me. I love you now and I always have, Allison. You mean just as much to me as Nova and Lyla do, and I want you and the kids to stay. Please. Read them."

He pushed the box even closer.

Allison thought of the way his eyes lit up when Chelsea met him at the door in the evenings, holding her arms up for him to swing her in the air. How he laughed at the crazy sounds that Toby made, or how he volunteered to help with the dirtiest diapers and the nighttime baths when she felt exhausted.

All of it as though making up for not doing those things for her.

Then she recalled how he'd cried when he'd come to the hotel, the fear in his eyes deep and frantic. The strength in his arms when he'd hugged each of them to his chest like he never wanted to let go.

She pushed the box back toward him.

His shoulders dropped and he turned to leave.

"Wait," she said.

He paused, his hand on the doorknob.

Allison pushed past all the past emotions of pain, of fear of rejection. She told herself that she wasn't bad luck, and that she only had to open her heart and take a chance.

Nate turned around, his eyes shiny with tears.

Then she spoke again, this time from the heart.

"I don't have to read them, Dad. I believe you. And, yes, if you'll have us, we'll stay."

A NOTE FROM THE AUTHOR:

Hello, readers! I hope you enjoyed *Blackbird*, the ninth book in the *Hart's Ridge* series. The true crime wrapped into the fictional town of Hart's Ridge and its fictional characters was loosely inspired by the hijacking and kidnapping of Alice Donovan. Lydia's story began in book eight, *Starting Over*, but, unlike the true crime in which Alice Donovan's body was finally found many years later, I decided to give Lydia another chance at being reunited with her family, and it just cannot fit in one or two books. Will that happen in the next book, *Hello Little Girl*? You'll have to read it and see!

Once more, my deepest condolences to the Donovan family, as well as other people who were victims of the Fulks and Basham crime spree.

Then we have Allison, a young mother who has met up with the wrong man not once, but twice. Her story was picked right out of my own memory bank. I left home at age sixteen and married a very abusive young man. After one incident, my father rented a house and hid me out there, but somehow my ex found it and was waiting there when we came home one evening. I spotted his car, and a high-speed chase ensued. My father drove us through red lights, over yards, and straight to the county sheriff's department, then lay on the horn until deputies came out and put my ex in handcuffs.

I was too terrified to press charges, and the judge told my father he'd hold the ex for twenty-four hours before letting him go. I threw everything into my car and drove straight through from South Carolina to Kansas and stayed with an uncle. My ex had no idea where I was until a family member told him. Long story short, he tracked me down and talked me into giving him another chance. I came back, we had a child, and I survived six more years of severe abuse before I got the courage to get away for good, this time on my own without help. Back then, no one ever told me there was such a thing as shelters for abused women. I wish I had known. If you know someone in an abusive relationship, please remind them there are options out there for help.

If you've enjoyed the nine books of Hart's Ridge, you'll be happy to know that I've decided to continue the series. Because of the huge popularity—and the ongoing love of the Gray family

—there are now 10. If you'd like to be notified when there is a new title and pre-order button, you can sign up for my monthly newsletter at the following link:

JOIN KAY'S NEWSLETTER HERE and Pre-Order book 10 Here. Keep reading to see the cover of HELLO LITTLE GIRL and read the description.

Besides this series, I have many more books for you to read! Check my author page on Amazon to see if you can find something that meets what you are looking for:

Kay Bratt's Amazon Author Page - I'd also like to invite you to join my private Facebook group, Kay's Krew, where you can be part of my focus group, giving ideas for story details such as names, livelihoods, sneak peeks, etc., in this series. I'm also known to entertain with stories of my life with the Bratt Pack and all the kerfuffle's I find myself getting into. Please join my author newsletter to hear of future Hart's Ridge books, as well as giveaways and discounts.

Until then,

Scatter kindness everywhere.

Kay Bratt

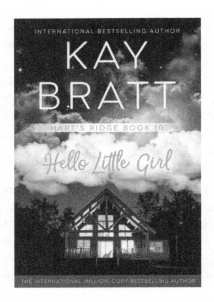

*Learn More about book ten in the *Hart's Ridge* series at this link: My Book In Hello Little Girl, book 10 of Hart's Ridge:

*IN THE PICTURESQUE **town of Hart's Ridge, where secrets linger and shadows dance, Deputy Taylor Gray finds herself at a crossroads in the much-anticipated tenth installment of the beloved small-town mystery series, "Hello Little Girl."***

TAYLOR IS GIVEN ALL she's ever wanted when her family is complete, but will it be enough to put them as priority and stop putting her career first?

MEANWHILE, a woman held in captivity grapples with a moral dilemma of her own. Trapped between the desire to reclaim her freedom and the urge to save another, she must summon the courage to make a choice that will shape not only her destiny but also the lives of those she holds dear.

JOIN DEPUTY TAYLOR GRAY and the resilient inhabitants of Hart's Ridge as they embark on a journey of self-discovery, redemption, and, ultimately, the triumph of the human spirit. *Hello Little Girl* promises to be a riveting addition to the series, leaving readers spellbound until the final revelation.

*LEARN MORE about book ten in the *Hart's Ridge* series at this link: My Book.

ABOUT THE AUTHOR

Kay Bratt learned to lean on writing while she navigated a tumultuous childhood and then a decade of domestic abuse in adulthood. After working her way through the hard years to come out a survivor and a pursuer of peace, she finally found the courage to use her experiences throughout her novels, most recently *Wish Me Home* and *True to Me*. Her books have fueled many exciting book club discussions and have made it into the hands of more than a million readers across the world. She lives with the love of her life and a pack of rescue dogs on the banks of Lake Hartwell in Georgia, USA.

For more information, visit www.kaybratt.com.

Made in United States
Orlando, FL
28 June 2025